FRATRICIDE
IS A GAS

LINDSAY GUTTERIDGE

FRATRICIDE
IS A GAS

JONATHAN CAPE
THIRTY BEDFORD SQUARE LONDON

FIRST PUBLISHED 1975
© 1975 BY LINDSAY GUTTERIDGE

JONATHAN CAPE LTD, 30 BEDFORD SQUARE, LONDON WCI

ISBN 0 224 01115 4

PRINTED IN GREAT BRITAIN BY
NORTHUMBERLAND PRESS LIMITED
GATESHEAD

To John Trevelyan

Nature averse to crime!
I tell you that nature lives
and breathes by it, hungers
at all her pores for bloodshed,
yearns with all her heart for
the furtherance of cruelty.

Marquis de Sade, 1792

PART ONE

1

OUT OF ORDER. It was the third day the notice had hung on the lift gate.

Bellamy flapped his wet umbrella and slowly climbed the concrete stairs, pulling on the iron handrail and pausing for breath between flights. Leaving the open umbrella in a corner of the big information room he entered his office.

He took from his pocket a metal sphere, as big as a tennis ball, and put it on his desk.

Mathew Dilke, controller of British micro-espionage, felt the shock of impact as the spherical transporter landed. He switched off the gyro-stabilizer, descended the ramp, walked out on to the desk top and looked around him.

The office was small. A green filing cabinet, a tin waste bin and a dark-wood-stained desk almost filled it. Outside the window a wall of glazed white bricks reflected dim light into the room, and the muffled sound of Ministry typewriters clacked up the brick air-shaft.

Bellamy had hung his coat behind the door. Dilke

heard the key turn and watched the big agent squeeze between cabinet and desk and sit down. The man sighed, removed heavy glasses, massaged his soft face with a plump hand, and replaced the glasses.

He stretched out and switched on his desk lamp and Dilke strode forward into the circle of light.

Mathew Dilke was a man nearing forty, with thinning hair and a high-bridged, arrogant nose. A muscular micro-man, a quarter of an inch tall,* who moved with nervy agility despite his heavy build. He stared up into Bellamy's huge face and waited for him to speak, impatient to know why he had been brought to London, away from his training camp.

Gilbert Bellamy glanced at the rain-streaked window then leaned forward and looked down at the microscopic figure on his desk.

'It's a foul day, Mathew. Sorry to drag you here in the middle of your training programme,' Bellamy raised a conciliatory hand, 'but his Lordship insisted on it.'

'We have a problem. Since the October signing of the germ warfare agreement, prohibiting stockpiling and bacteriological warfare research, free inspection on both sides of the curtain has been rigorous enough to make the treaty stand up. But the agreement only covers the main Eastern and Western blocs; the Government was aware that research could go on elsewhere and accepted this as unavoidable, but now we suspect that Russia is buying freelance research information in Peru. A report we've had from Lima seems to confirm this.' Bellamy paused. 'Lord Raglen wants you to go out there and check it.'

Bellamy opened a drawer, took out a folder and dropped it on the desk. Dilke staggered in the rush of

* Dilke stands below de Sade – page 6

disturbed air. 'I'd like your views on my plan for the trip.'

'But first we must make contact.' He pulled again at the drawer, which stuck half way. He cursed amiably, groped in its dark interior, then withdrew his hand. Two objects lay in the great palm: a blue plastic box $1\frac{1}{2}$ inches by $1\frac{1}{2}$ inches by $\frac{1}{2}$ inch and, linked to it by twin cables, a flesh-coloured earplug.

'The very latest thing in deaf aids!'

Bellamy set down the box. It rocked on its narrow base and fell forward with a crash. The desk jarred beneath Dilke's feet.

'Jesus!' said Dilke.

Bellamy righted the box and laid a forefinger on its rounded top. 'You can speak to me from this observation dome.' He raised the plug to his left ear and looked down expectantly at Dilke.

Afraid that the box might fall again Dilke cautiously approached it from the side. He slid open a door and entered a brightly-lit shaft. He went up a steel ladder at a fast climb, and came out into the observation chamber.

A swivel chair fitted with body harness stood beneath the transparent dome. The floor and the chair were dark blue, and a matching blue cat-suit lay across the chair-back. Dilke could see no microphone.

Outside, the huge figure sat in patient repose, elbow on desk, head propped on the hand which held the earplug.

'Hello!' Dilke called.

Gilbert Bellamy winced and pulled the plug from his ear. The acre of pink face began to move, the great cheeks expanded, swelling the pouches beneath the half-closed eyes; between the fingerprint patterns on top of the dome Dilke watched the corners of the mouth stretch up in an enormous slow smile.

'Hello, Mathew. You are loud and clear. I'll lower the volume.'

A hand came quickly over the edge of the desk and loomed above the container.

'Wait!'

The hand remained poised. The smile behind it vanished.

'I'll lower my voice. Let me get strapped in before we go any further.'

He sat down and buckled the harness then spoke quietly to the microphone grille in the arm of the chair.

'O.K.'

The hand approached more circumspectly. Dilke braced his feet against the foot bar as the thumb and fingers closed on the box with ponderous delicacy. The transporter sailed up at a steep angle and was lowered into Bellamy's breast pocket and clipped on to the pocket edge. The plug was taken from the desk and pressed into a huge ear. Fingers concealed the flex beneath the lapel, looped up the excess cable and tucked it inside the jacket collar. Then Bellamy absent-mindedly tapped the pocket with the flat of his hand and Dilke was thrown hard against the chair straps.

'Christ!'

'Damnation! I'm sorry.'

Dilke leaned back and looked up. The huge eyes blinked down through thick lenses and the mouth formed a vast, penitent curve.

Dilke shook his head wearily. 'All right, Gilbert. No bones broken. There is grease on the dome, can you clean it please?'

Gilbert Bellamy's hands hovered before the transporter, 'The cover unclips . . . I can remove it to clean it.'

'No! A rub with your handkerchief will do.'

The vast torso slowly tilted, the right hand fished in a trouser pocket and produced a crumpled handkerchief. It was spread like a tarpaulin on the desk below and Dilke watched the enormous hands fold and press it into a thick, square pad. One hand cupped the breast pocket and the other rubbed the pad back and forth over the perspex cover; the fingerprint smeared and gradually disappeared; a few dust particles, caught by static electricity, danced upon the shining dome.

'Right, Gilbert. Let's see this plan.'

Bellamy shook out the handkerchief and polished his spectacle lenses.

Bellamy's plan was simple and direct.

The suspect laboratories in Peru belonged to a plastics manufacturer. To give Dilke access to the laboratories Bellamy (posing as the director of an investment company) proposed to visit the Peruvian manufacturer to acquire patent rights.

'Our ambassador in Lima can fix up an introduction for me.'

'That might look suspicious,' objected Dilke.

'On the contrary! Salesmanship and diplomacy go hand-in-hand in Latin America; the Foreign Office has always encouraged trading relations out there.'

'All right, Gilbert. The plan in outline seems fine, but before we go any further,' Dilke's voice was cold, 'why have I been dragged away from training camp when I have a dozen micro-agents who could do this job?'

'Lord Raglen has asked for you specifically.'

'I know,' Dilke said shortly. 'But why?'

'It is precisely because you *are* in charge of micro-training that he wants you to go. The most crucial, and the least satisfactory part of our micro-espionage system is delivering agents to and recovering them from areas of investigation. This Peruvian job will give us the chance to evolve a method which you can train your men to use.'

Bellamy sat back and solemnly folded his great hands across the curve of his stomach. 'We must face the fact that we have no monopoly of miniaturization. Knowledge of it has got around, it is an open secret in the scientific world. We know that Russia has micro-agents. We can stay ahead only by devising effective delivery and recovery systems.' Bellamy paused. 'We have an audience with his lordship tomorrow, to receive his blessing,' he smiled fatly. 'You can argue with him then if you wish.'

'All right, Gilbert.' Dilke had been angered by the abrupt interruption of his supervision of the micro-training course. Now his ill humour faded. The mission was clearly important and he recognized the value of being personally involved. And the chance of escaping from his desk job and exchanging English fogs for Peruvian sunshine was not unattractive.

'How will this delivery/recovery system of yours work?'

'You will work from a base. Think of it in terms of space exploration, of a spaceship which can move freely to and from a bigger ship.'

'So I'm to be your satellite?'

'Don't misunderstand, Mathew.' Bellamy added smoothly, 'The mission is in your hands; I will have a passive role. Look on me,' Bellamy smiled, 'as your Trojan horse. There are cameras and tape machines in the hearing aid with which you can record the information. I will get you as near to its source as I can, then the rest is up to you.'

'With my little camera and tape recorder?'

'Yes.'

'Gilbert. This is essentially the same as *macro-espionage*! Intelligence agents have been dropping bugged olives into Martinis and sneaking shots with tie-pin cameras ever since the transistor was invented.'

'No, no. This is different. With conventional bugging the agent has to get very close to the source of information, otherwise he can't plant the device. It is often impossible. But you can go where I can't, *you* will have mobility ...'

'So I'll be a sort of bug on two legs?'

Bellamy slowly shrugged his great shoulders. 'You *could* put it that way.'

Dilke smiled for the first time.

He had a lot of homework to do. He needed knowledge of bacteriological warfare: 'I wouldn't know a germ weapon if I was sitting on it.' And he needed background information about Peru, the plastics factory, the people running it, and why their activities were suspect.

'I think you'll find answers to most of your questions in your office files, Mathew. They're on the floor below you, but I'll get more information if you need it.'

Bellamy replaced the hearing aid on the desk to give it stability and Dilke went below decks ... the Aid had a marked nautical character with its metal ladder and hatchway to the observation platform.

He started at the bottom of the shaft and did a quick reconnaissance of the transporter. There were three decks below the observation chamber: a water tank and a one-volt battery filled the bottom deck; living quarters, with a cabin, galley and bathroom, were on the next deck; and the office, wireless room and stores were on the third one.

Dilke opened doors and cupboards at random and found a hatch in the end wall of the office which gave access to a transparent globe about five millimetres in dimeter (five micro-feet to Dilke) and which contained a chair like the one in the observation chamber. The duplication of the chair was puzzling. Gilbert Bellamy's room was visible through the transparent walls of the globe; he saw Bellamy dropping a huge square sack of tea into a cup as big as a gasometer. Then he closed the hatch, looked for the files and found four drawersful of them packed with indexed folders: 'Biowar' (shorthand for biological, alias bacteriological warfare). 'Peru': sub-divided into its geography, its politics, its industry. 'Plastics': from raw material to manufactured products. 'Personalities': a *Who's Who* of everyone connected with the mission.

A thick file labelled 'THE AID' gave an exhaustive description of the hearing-aid transporter. Dilke skimmed through its contents; he had used camouflaged transporters before (a cigarette pack and a matchbox*) but the Aid was far in advance of them. The micro-engineering department had been given its head and produced a little miracle of compact design, filled with sophisticated equipment.

The equipment list filled many sheets: clothing, climbing gear, food (nothing in the way of drink – he made a mental note), weapons, movie and still cameras, a pocket sound-recorder, a torch, a phone tapper and hook-up (to be used, parasite fashion, to make calls through a full-size telephone). Micro-technology had

* See *Cold War in a Country Garden* and *Killer Pine*.

14

moved on since his first clumsy radio-telephone!

This whole plan must have been in preparation for months. He slammed the drawers shut, annoyed that he hadn't been told about it before.

He would return to the files later, first he needed a broad picture, a framework into which this mass of detail would fit. He left the office, climbed the ladder to the top deck, sat back under the dome and waited for Bellamy to finish his tea.

Bellamy had briefed Dilke on a job once before, and the micro-agent had discovered a sharp and complex intelligence behind the man's ponderous exterior.

Bellamy was in his fifties. He had started in military intelligence during the war (wearing a beret in occupied France and radioing Nazi troop movements to London) and was given a job in the information department when the war ended. His transition from the drama of field work to the tedium of desk work was marked by a number of incidents which had become part of the folklore of the department. Dilke recollected, with a smile, the Victoria Station story: while awaiting a train after some seasonal celebration, Bellamy had contrived a 'dog-collar' from a strip of card and delivered an impromptu sermon on the evils of drink from a luggage truck (subsequent embroidery had added the spending of a silver collection in the station bar). The incident, combined with Bellamy's naturally episcopal manner, had earned him the title of Bishop. The nickname had fallen into disuse over the years and Bellamy's taste for burlesque had faded, but his quirky imagination found another and more prosaic outlet.

Bellamy became an armchair spy. He worked in the small, smoke-filled office next to the information room (filled from floor to ceiling with racks of newspapers and magazines), sifting through the world's press for significant news of enemy activities. Bellamy brought to the job analytical ability, a retentive memory and a formidable linguistic talent; but it was his nimble imagination which made him an armchair spy of genius. He spent his days in a haze of free-association, juggling snippets of news, in a dozen different languages, into dazzling hypothetical structures which his colleagues carried away to test and explore.

Bellamy finished his tea and lit a cigarette, then blinked down myopically at the still figure sitting under the dome.

Mathew Dilke's face was a featureless spot, small as the dot on an i, against the dark observation platform. They had never met before Dilke's miniaturization and Bellamy's mental picture of the micro-man derived from a service photograph in his dossier: Dilke posed on a tank with his grinning crew; slim muscular torso burnt almost black by the sun, goggles on forehead, thin unsmiling face staring at the camera.

The photograph was almost twenty years out of date. Dilke's body was thickset now and his narrow, arched nose jutted from an older, broader face.

The dossier covered his career from tank-corps captaincy to his command of micro-espionage. It credited him with resilience, resourcefulness and a high I.Q., and debited him with arrogance and a low-flashpoint temper. In action he had displayed an aggressive, sometimes foolhardy courage which was not exceptional in young officers. But to have accepted, in his maturity, the role of guinea-pig in the first experiments in miniaturization, showed a sort of courage which Gilbert Bellamy respected but could not comprehend. To Bellamy, the insect world made large was the ultimate horror, and Dilke had been the first Englishman to face it. But beneath the respect he felt for Mathew Dilke, lurked another feeling: an irrational, sneaking fear of this minute and uncannily concentrated intelligence.

Bellamy shivered, then smiled and lifted the earplug to his ear.

Dilke spoke immediately: 'The word for your files is *voluminous*, Gilbert.'

'I hope you're happy with them.'

'Too much to take in yet. I'd like to see Porton, and I'd better see a plastics factory before we fly to Lima: I need to know the difference between their labs.'

'I'll fix that immediately. We have our date with Lord Raglen tomorrow, I'll arrange some visits for after that.'

2

Dilke sat in the Aid 1,500 micro-feet above the floor, isolated from the micro-world where man's giant actions (the crash of a cup in saucer, slam of drawer in desk, scrape of chair on floor) caused ceaseless tremors and quakes.

The shock of Bellamy's footsteps was absorbed by his vast bulk and smoothed into a series of breathtaking wavelike movements. Dilke moved as if riding through the aftermath of a titanic storm, feeling a mixture of nausea and exhilaration as he saw the walls of the corridor fly past.

Bellamy walked along passages, descended two flights of stone steps to the ground floor, climbed a carpeted stairway and went along the wide corridor which led to Raglen's room. He knocked on double-doors then passed through them and walked steadily towards two men who waited for him at the end of a long room.

Light from chandeliers and tall fog-enshrouded windows yellowed the velvet curtains and walls, shone dimly on the varnished features of Joseph Chamberlain who stood in a ten-foot gilded frame above an Adam fire-place, and gleamed on Lord Raglen's polished bald head.

Raglen watched Gilbert Bellamy's approach with his habitual expression of frigid ill-humour. He nodded acknowledgment of Bellamy's good morning, nodded at the hearing aid in the agent's pocket and asked, 'Have you got Captain Dilke?' Then he introduced the man who stood at his side.

'This is Sir James Jebb, our Ambassador in Peru. As he's here on a visit I've asked him to tell you about this germ-war business.'

Both men were of middle height and portly build, but the Ambassador to Peru was less sombrely dressed than the head of British Military Intelligence: opal cuff-links as big as pigeon's eggs and the soft silk folds of a display handkerchief in the breast pocket of his grey lounge suit betrayed an insidious Latin influence. Sir James's hair was swept back in wings over his ears, and he wore the practised smile of a career diplomat. He gave Bellamy a firm handshake and stared with frank curiosity into the observation chamber of the Aid; then they sat down at the end of the long board-room table.

'What can I tell you, Mr Bellamy?'

'We would like to know the reasons for suspecting that illicit research is going on, Sir James.'

'You understand, Mr Bellamy, that all we have are suspicions?' The ambassador began cautiously. 'We have no hard facts to go on.'

'Of course, Sir James. Our job is to look into the sources of your suspicions.'

'Perhaps I should begin with the background and work back to the suspicions ...'

'Just as you wish, Sir James.'

The ambassador sat back and cleared his throat portentously.

'Since the present government of Peru came into power it has made considerable adjustments to its relationships with other countries, though I may say, in parenthesis,' Jebb half-turned and smiled at Lord Raglen, 'that our own friendship with Peru has remained unimpaired. Peru's expropriation of American-owned oil fields and refineries and its subsequent dispute with the United States has encouraged Soviet Russia to make strenuous commercial overtures to Peru. Russian trade fairs have been held in Lima and Russian trade delegations have toured Peruvian civil and industrial organizations, including the organization which is under suspicion.'

'*What* is the suspicion, Gilbert?' Dilke asked. Bellamy blinked but did not interrupt the ambassador.

'The firm is called Compañía Peruana de Plásticos and is controlled by a man called Lippe: a queer character who took over the business in mysterious circumstances two years ago and has not been seen outside the premises since.'

'Ask him for the evidence that they are making biological weapons,' interjected Dilke.

'And you think that this man Lippe is involved in biological weapon making, Sir James?' Bellamy asked.

'I know that a member of the Russian delegation which visited C.P.P. was a Soviet colonel in civilian clothes,' the ambassador said slowly.

'And he could have been buying plastic rocket-kits!' Dilke said tersely. 'All this is bloody tenuous, Gilbert.'

'Captain Dilke feels that the evidence so far is rather tenuous, Sir James.' Bellamy smiled, 'I must confess that I see his point, after all it is not uncommon for members of the Russian armed forces to travel incognito with civilian parties.'

Lord Raglen, who had been sitting with his eyes fixed on the Aid, interrupted abruptly.

'Captain Dilke, Sir James Jebb was about to tell you the most significant part of his story. The laboratories of Compañía Peruana de Plásticos are being supplied with mules. This is a most curious fact, Captain Dilke. Mules and plastics do not go together; on the other hand, mules are frequently used in the production of vaccines and it is conceivable that they are being used in Peru for the incubation of bacteria. Soviet military presence at this factory may or may not be of special significance but I am satisfied that an activity other than the manufacture of plastics is taking place there and I want it investigated.'

Bellamy spoke again after a short silence.

'I have cabled your commercial office in Lima, Sir James, asking for an introduction to C.P.P. and I will be grateful if you can discreetly speed up the introduction.'

'I have always been a passionate advocate of close business ties between the United Kingdom and Latin America and I am sure that your request for an introduction will be attended to with all speed, Mr Bellamy; but I will speak to my commercial secretary and stress the urgency of the matter.'

The interview seemed to be at an end; Bellamy glanced at Lord Raglen, received a nod of dismissal and made his stately way from the room and back to his office.

Dilke was irked by his need to rely on Bellamy as a spokesman and interpreter. He had a day in hand before a visit to a plastics factory in Kent so he vacated the Aid and sent it back to the engineers with instructions to re-jig its communications system.

He camped in the big spherical giro-transporter on Bellamy's desk and read the armful of files which he had abstracted from the Aid.

Republica del Peru: a right-wing dictatorship run by General Fernando de la Fuenté (listed under PERSONALITIES) covering an area ten times the size of England; situated on the west side of equatorial South America. Geography: a central spine of mountains with dense forest-lands to the east and barren coastal plains to the west. Climate: hot dry days and cold nights, with clammy coastal fogs.

Capital city: Lima, near the coast, with a population of two million (original Inca capital: Cuzco, built high in the Andes from monumental granite blocks).

Total population: ten million: three-quarters Indian, one-eighth Spanish, the rest Indo-Spanish, and a few Japanese.

There were pages more; about products and resources, currency, religion, education, sport. Dilke skimmed through them and came to

Compañia Peruana de Plásticos: registered as a limited company in the business archives at Lima. Offices, laboratories, factory and quarries are situated 70 kilometres east of Lima. The company processes plastic raw material and manufactures plastic goods; it also does an international trade in raw plastic (listed under PLASTICS).

Chairman and Managing Director: **Professor** Heinrich Lippe (listed under PERSONALITIES).

The files on 'Plastics' and 'Personalities' were both in the Aid. Dilke closed the Peruvian file and walked out on to the desk.

Gilbert Bellamy lay back in his chair, silently smoking a cigarette and gazing at the wall of white bricks outside his window. He sat with his great hands folded across his stomach, one eye shut against the stream of smoke which drifted up along the side of his nose. The telephone rang, and an avalanche of ash tumbled down the slopes of his waistcoat as he reached for it.

Dilke watched him as he negotiated a visit to Porton Down Microbiological Research Laboratories. Bellamy's air of well-fed authority fitted him for the role of British businessman which he was soon to adopt, but his rather worn shirt-collar and cuffs and rumpled suit suggested that his business was not booming.

Bellamy arranged for the visit to Porton to follow their trip to the Kentish plastics factory and spent the remainder of the day on routine office affairs. Dilke watched him from the shadow of the giro-transporter and walked on the desk in the twilight of evening after his companion had gone home.

When the Aid was returned next day, Dilke's listed modifications had all been made: additional microphones allowed him to speak to Bellamy from the Aid's living quarters and office as well as from the observation chamber; the transmitter's volume range had been dramatically increased so that his voice could be heard even when he was not directly plugged in to Bellamy's ear; extra grab-rails had been installed on all decks, the ladder in the shaft was enclosed in a steel-mesh safety cage, and a case of Scotch had been added to his stock of provisions.

The booster which gave extra volume was linked with the observation-chamber microphone, and to ensure that Bellamy's eardrum would not be inadvertently blasted, it could be activated only by sustained pressure on a lever in the arm of the chair.

They tried it out with the earplug lying beside the Aid on the desk top. Dilke sat in the chair, pressed the lever and slowly and deliberately counted to ten. The amplified voice which came from the earplug was high-pitched and scratchy but quite audible.

They were both delighted. Dilke recited a limerick and sang a snatch of song which Bellamy conducted with a massive forefinger, then he installed the Aid in his pocket and fitted the plug into his ear. Dilke sat strapped into his seat ready for the journey to Kent and saw worn threads on the edge of the pocket, sprouting like weeds in a window box.

'You will make a threadbare financier, Gilbert. I know a tailor in Cork Street who can make you a suit in forty-eight hours; something conservative and sincere in blue pinstripe, I think ...'

A company car met the train from London at Sevenoaks, and took them along lanes which wound between regimented forests of bare hop-poles to the factory. They arrived in time for Bellamy to have lunch in the management dining-room (all oak panels and wrought-iron wall lamps) with a public relations man, who then took them on a tour of the plant, displaying gay cordiality towards a surly workforce en route, and enthusiastically spouting output figures as they watched machines consuming raw plastic and discharging finished products.

'Ask to see the labs, Gilbert,' Dilke said.

'I'd like to see your laboratories,' Bellamy shouted through the thunder of fluorescent-yellow buckets bouncing out of the maw of a huge German bucket-making machine. ('We can't always *get* the machinery we want in the U.K. ...')

He was taken to the office of the technical director, a tall, dark, cynical man in a white coat called Pyke, who gave him a child's guide to plastics.

'Bubble-gum is a plastic, Mr Bellamy. So are table-jellies, gold-bars, and concrete motorways. At some stage in their manufacture they are all malleable, the differences between them are differences of material and of durability ...'

The P.R. man left the room and returned with beakers of vending-machine coffee.

'... It is all a question of molecules. Industrial plastics have long-chain giant molecules which can be formed by heat and pressure into an article as big as a ship's hull or as small as,' the director tapped his beaker with a pencil, 'a disposable coffee cup.'

'Raw plastic is extracted chiefly from coal and oil, though casein and cellulose – milk and cotton – are used on a small scale for specialized products ...'

Pyke showed Bellamy his laboratories and explained, with an increasing use of technical terms, the purposes of the laboratory equipment.

'Do you do much experimental work, Mr Pyke?'

'All the time. But my main job is quality control.'

'Ask him if he's heard of the Peruvian firm,' prompted Dilke.

'Have you heard of a South American firm called Compañía Peruana de Plásticos, Mr Pyke?'

'We buy material from them.'

'You have probably heard of Professor Lippe, then.'

The technical director cocked an eyebrow. 'Yes, I know of Lippe. His chemical research work is well known. He is a great innovator; by combining petrochemicals and minerals he has created a range of plastics with unique properties, which is why we buy from him.'

Bellamy nodded brightly and Pyke was encouraged to go on. 'The basic mineral which Lippe uses is a type of volcanic rock found only on the western seaboard of South America and he has exclusive rights in Peru to mine it.' An ironic smile curled Pyke's lip. 'So he is not only clever, he's as rich as hell!'

Gilbert Bellamy laughed and passed smoothly on to other subjects, and when Dilke told him that he had seen enough Bellamy took his leave and was driven through misty lanes to catch a train home.

Next morning Gilbert Bellamy drove his old Rover through a fine drizzle to Porton Down.

He went via Staines, driving carefully on the wet roads and sedately overtaking juggernauts on the A.30.

The gates in the wire fence which surrounded the Porton establishment had been opened and he drove into the big staff parking lot and parked alongside a solitary car. The drizzle changed to a downpour as he left his car, and he hurried up a shallow flight of steps into the squat, red-brick building – bouncing Dilke in his seat – and dashed rain from his hat in the entrance hall.

Only the distant gruff bark of a dog broke the silence, then a shutter in the facing wall slid back revealing a small bald man with a dreary moustache.

'Mr Bellamy?'

'Yes,' Bellamy replied.

'From Whitehall?'

'From Whitehall.'

'To see Professor Ruttlidge?'

'To see Professor Ruttlidge,' Bellamy intoned sonorously.

The shutter closed, the little man, now wearing a peaked cap, came through a door and led the way down a dark corridor.

The door to the professor's office was open and Ruttlidge sat at his desk with his hands deep in his overcoat pockets, wearing a hat, and muffled to the ears in a woollen scarf. He had a long, sad face and was suffering from a heavy cold. He shook hands, shut the door and waved Bellamy to a seat.

'You said on the phone that you wanted to look over the labs, Mr Bellamy. There's not much to see I'm afraid; there's nothing going on here, Porton has been closed down since last October.'

'Yes, Professor, but I believe there is still equipment here and I hoped that you would give me an idea of the work you were engaged on.'

'Surely, Mr Bellamy. In the time available I can give you only a superficial understanding of our work.' Ruttlidge dabbed tenderly at his nose with a sodden handkerchief, 'But I'll do my best to answer your questions.'

'Can you start with the reason for Porton Down's existence?'

'Porton was established in 1916 to develop war gases. After the Second World War investigations were made here into methods of biological warfare, to enable this country to defend itself against microbiological weapons.'

'The problem is to draw a line between defence and attack, I suppose, Professor.'

'That is so, Mr Bellamy; all countries which ran biological warfare programmes claimed to do so for reasons of defence. Defence must be based on knowledge of the weapons and how they are produced. Once a country has this knowledge, actual production is not difficult; in fact any commercial pharmaceutical laboratory can be quickly adapted to weapon-making.'

'And what is the prime objective of a biological weapons manufacturer?'

Ruttlidge gazed lugubriously across his bare desk. 'Biological war has been defined as "public health in reverse", Mr Bellamy. The job of a weapons maker is to find a micro-organism which is stable, virulent, highly infective and capable of speedy production by mass-production methods ...'

'Can you carry on this talk in the laboratories, Gilbert?' Dilke said. 'I must relate all this to laboratory hardware.'

At Bellamy's request they left the office, walked dry-shod through shallow troughs which had once contained germicide, and entered an area of dim corridors and laboratories; Ruttlidge continued his exposition as they passed between long rows of empty germ-culture tanks.

'There is no perfect bacterial weapon because each strain of bacteria has its deficiencies: man has considerable immunity to some diseases; antibiotics and vaccines are effective against others; and there are diseases which are so long lived that they are militarily unacceptable, for an infected enemy country could not soon be occupied; the anthrax bacillus, for instance, can lie dormant in the soil for a hundred years.'

'You make it all sound pretty futile, Professor.'

'Oh no! In practice enemy territory would be blanketed with a mixture of diseases which would be effective

28

in combination, and the victims would display such conflicting symptoms that medical diagnosis – and therefore treatment – would be made difficult. However, an international search for a single perfect bacteriological weapon has been going on for years. Perhaps *search* is the wrong word, because no suitable strain of bacteria exists. A new strain must be *artificially created* to fulfil the demands of the military specification.'

'Follow this up, Gilbert,' Dilke said.

Bellamy smiled. 'If you will forgive my saying so, Professor Ruttlidge, that sounds like a job for Dr Frankenstein.'

'Not at all! The project is perfectly feasible. In fact it is my view that it was the imminent success of our work here at Porton which forced Russia to sign the October treaty.' Ruttlidge tapped the nearest stainless-steel tank. 'Right up to the moment of signature we were working on a strain of pneumonic plague which showed great promise.'

'It all sounds *incredibly* complicated.'

Dilke gazed through the observation dome and detected a gleam of self-satisfaction in the professor's watery eye. 'It requires a combination of scientific techniques and a great deal of time and money.' Ruttlidge launched into analogy, 'Producing a virulent strain of bacteria is like breeding belligerence into fighting bulls: a continuous process of culling is necessary to attain perfection. We have raised families of micro-organisms of up to a million consecutive generations in these tanks.' He smoothed the gleaming steel with a pale hand.

'Have you ever used living animals like horses and mules and cows as germ incubators, Professor?' Bellamy asked.

'There *are* some advantages in using such animals, but

we found it convenient to grow bacteria in culture mediums of minced chicken embryos, which can then be irradiated to encourage mutation. We used lung tissue as the medium for the pneumonic plague project as it is a respiratory disease.

'We have used animals to test results and we have a farm which breeds rodents for that purpose.'

'And what has happened to your farm?'

'It is still in operation; great numbers of animals are supplied to commercial laboratories.'

The test area was a complex of rooms with low ceilings, containing avenues of empty cages. They stopped here and there to read slips of card slotted into the cage-fronts: here a batch of rats had been undergoing cholera tests; here mice had been injected with smallpox; here rabbits had been given syphilis.

'Have you ever feared a possible doomsday effect from all this, Professor Ruttlidge? Could not large-scale epidemics be released into the world accidentally?'

'There is no risk-free activity in this world, Mr Bellamy. The media made a fuss about the risks involved, but in fact they were minimal, and one had to balance them against the risk that unfriendly powers would leave us behind in this vital field of research.'

Bellamy nodded a judicious agreement.

'And there is a parallel between a biological weapon and the hydrogen bomb,' Ruttlidge persisted. 'The existence of such devastating weapons deters countries from going to war.'

Bellamy nodded again. Grey light filtered through the windows and illuminated the thousands of cages with their open wire gates. A pungent odour of Lysol rose from the damp concrete floor. The air was cold.

'I think we've finished here,' Dilke said.

'Thank you very much, Professor Ruttlidge. I'm very grateful. I've learnt a great deal.'

They retraced their steps to the administrative sector, and as they stood in the entrance hall Bellamy smiled and asked his last question, 'And what are you busy on now, Professor?'

'I am research director at a pharmacological firm, working on a contraceptive pill for men ...'

The shutter which covered the wall-hatch shot open and the bald-headed man and a Dobermann Pinscher with its paws on the ledge stared ŏut.

'All right, Caretaker,' said Ruttlidge, 'I have something to collect from my office, then I will be leaving.'

Bellamy shook hands with him and pushed through the plate-glass doors.

'From plague and the pox to the pill,' Dilke said as Bellamy descended the steps, 'the professor is a bit of a specialist in population control.'

He felt Bellamy's vast silent laugh.

'*Could* his plague have affected the signing of the treaty, Gilbert?'

'Possibly. It may have been used as blackmail. But I suspect the professor's opinion is coloured by his self-esteem.'

Bellamy drove out on to the main road; the rain had stopped and a transient ray of sunshine was reflected dazzlingly from the wet tarmac. Dilke squinted up through the observation chamber dome.

'Tomorrow we shall transform you into a City gent, Gilbert.'

In the window of Solomon and Bostock a plumed and polished military helmet rested resplendently on bolts of light blue, dark blue and khaki serge. Eye-level curtains across the back of the window gave some privacy to the shop's interior and concealment to the man who stood behind them gazing across Cork Street at an exhibition of Picasso nymphs and satyrs.

A taxi pulled up outside, obscuring the display of rampant sexuality, and Gilbert Bellamy alighted and made his way to the entrance of the shop. The tailor approached him, gently massaging one palm with the other, and wished him good morning.

'Good morning! My name is Bellamy; Captain Mathew Dilke recommended that I should come to you, I need a business suit in rather a hurry. Are you Mr Bostock?'

'I am Mr Solomon, sir; but I remember Captain Dilke very well.' Solomon's hands flew apart then came together again in pious regret. 'I am afraid Mr Bostock died last year, sir, of a sudden heart attack. I have taken my son into partnership.'

He led Bellamy to a fitting-room at the rear of the shop to be measured, and chatted as he wrote down the figures murmured to him by his son, a doleful man approaching middle-age.

Dilke watched from the pocket of Bellamy's jacket which had been put on a hanger and hung on a coat-rack.

'I trust that Captain Dilke is well, Mr Bellamy. He is an old customer of ours, but it is some years since he last visited us. I thought, perhaps, that he had left the country.'

'Oh, he's fine. I see quite a bit of him ...'

Bellamy stood with upraised arms as Solomon junior encircled his generous waist with a tape-measure.

'The Captain is still in London; in fact he is working not so very far from here,' he added solemnly.

Bellamy asked for a single vent in the jacket, pockets with flaps, and no turn-ups; then he picked a discreet pinstripe and left with a firm promise that the suit would be ready in two days.

He bought cuff-links and a pigskin cigar-case in Old Bond Street, replaced his battered Omega and its worn wrist-strap at Asprey's, and returned home with a dozen hand-made shirts from Simpson's.

Dilke waited until the door of the Pimlico flat closed behind them then spoke tersely into the Aid's microphone, 'Solomon must have thought it bloody funny that you could hear perfectly well without your hearing aid!'

The elation which Bellamy had felt after his shopping spree vanished in a moment. He stood quite still, then sank back into a chair and closed his eyes.

Dilke watched the colour rise in his companion's cheeks; after a long silence he grunted and spoke again.

'There is a lot to do in the next two days. Check that Jebb has fixed the visit to C.P.P. and sort out the flight details, and you will need to pick up your suit. I need some peace and quiet to study the files and familiarize myself with the gear on board the Aid, so I'll stay here when you go to the office. I can attach a miniature dialler and phone-tapper to your phone here if we need to make contact. Is there anything else you can think of?'

Bellamy said quietly and slowly, 'Just that I promise it won't happen again.'

Dilke laughed dryly, 'I think you'd better make that earplug a permanent fixture: awake and asleep!'

At bedtime Bellamy stood the Aid on his bedside table and placed the coiled flex and the earplug beside it.

A clock and Bellamy's new watch close by made a shattering counterpoint of sound. Dilke called to Bellamy through the Aid speaker and Bellamy moved them both to the mantelshelf before going to bed.

Dilke descended to his living quarters and ate, then went to the office, pulled open a drawer and took out the first file.

3

After forty hours' ceaseless work, Dilke had read the files and had familiarized himself with every item of equipment on board the Aid.

When Bellamy came home with the new suit on the evening of the second day, he did a full dress-rehearsal of his role as entrepreneur, strolling round the flat wreathed in cigar smoke. Then he relaxed in an arm-chair with a gin big enough to fill a swimming pool, and Dilke sat in his swivel-chair with his legs crossed, drinking Scotch whisky.

Dilke had discovered the purpose of the second chair and the transparent globe which enclosed it. The globe was the head of a fake mapping pin, which could be detached from the side of the Aid and surreptitiously left, with himself inside, anywhere information might be found.

They tried it out. Dilke entered the head of the pin through the hatch in the office wall, and Bellamy wandered round the flat with a gin in one hand and the pin in the other, bending to stick it in skirting-boards and stretching to stick it in picture rails. The ride was dizzyingly erratic but the seat was on gimbals and remained level at all times.

They discussed its merits and its use.

'If I wished to reconnoitre, a skirting-board would be an ideal site. I could use it as a pathway round a room.'

'It's an ingenious idea, Mathew, but I can see snags. Recovering it might be a problem, and spot-on timing would be essential. If I picked it up prematurely you'd be left high and dry.'

'Wear shoes with laces, Gilbert. Bending to tie a lace would allow you to plant the pin without it being noticed.'

Their plane was due to leave Heathrow at seven next morning and Bellamy went early to bed; but though Dilke had not slept for almost two days he felt no desire for sleep. The weariness which he had felt earlier had gone, as if he had passed through a fatigue barrier, and now he was restless and keyed-up.

He ate a meal, then returned to the top deck. Bellamy had thoughtlessly left his wristwatch on the bedside table; but without the bass accompaniment of the alarm clock its tick was less disturbing than before. The huge steel watchcase and wristband of braided steel gleamed faintly in stray light from a lamp in the street outside. It was a waterproof, shockproof, self-winding, expensive watch, with a calendar, a tachometer and a lapsed-time bezel. Dilke checked his own watch against it. They synchronized. It was almost midnight.

He gazed at Gilbert Bellamy's sprawling bulk and listened to his deep, slow breathing, and he thought about their relationship.

The nausea he had felt when travelling for the first time in the Aid had been followed by a feeling of ex-hilaration. The Aid was the control centre of a vast flesh and blood machine, running on pure oxygen and powered by a heart like an enormous twin diesel and Dilke recognized that the control which he exercised over it was a part of his exhilaration.

But a subtle change was taking place between them. Dilke had experienced occasional, odd sensations of unreality as he was carried through the corridors of Whitehall and the streets of London. From the Aid he viewed the world from normal height, and moved through it at normal speed; and there were moments when he lost a sense of his true size. It was as if he had returned to the normality of his life before miniaturization ... or as if, for fleeting moments, there was a fusion between the micro- and the macro-worlds which he and Gilbert Bellamy inhabited.

Bellamy sighed and murmured and turned over. The bed, the floor, the table, the Aid moved; as if the earth had shifted in its sleep.

Dilke stared at the huge, dim shape.

Might his indefinable and shadowy feelings be the signs of a strange, new, symbiotic relationship between man and micro-man? Was this the birth of a dual human being? Each part an extension of the other?

Dilke shook his head impatiently. It was all too bloody fanciful for words. He walked to the viewing seat and sat down and turned his thoughts to the realities of their mission.

The litany of diseases which he had found in the file on 'Biowar' danced through his mind.

Melioidosis, brucellosis, syphilis, scarlatina, variola. Words like the names of flowers, concealing the dreadful realities of vomiting, diarrhoea, boils, lesions, gangrenous rashes, and death. The compiler of the file had devised a points system of effectiveness (Ruttlidge's plague was a Best Buy) and had made theoretical excursions into the possibilities of breeding hybrid strains of bacteria.

Dilke's face was stiff with disgust. Anything he could do to stop this barbarous investment in suffering, he would do.

The file on Heinrich Lippe had been surprisingly thick. The bulk of it was a micro-filmed dossier from the records of the Allied War Crimes Tribunal, and was an account of his life up to the end of the war.

Lippe was half-German, half-Swiss. He had been a brilliant and industrious student and graduate who had written notable papers on a variety of subjects: biology, geology, chemistry, etc. Wartime service as a research chemist at the Regierung Laboratories (where death-camp gases were manufactured) had brought him before the Tribunal.

The court decided that he was an academic scientist, interested only in pure research (the dossier photograph showed a man with a mop of unruly hair and an abstracted expression on his face) who had taken no part in the Führer's Final Solution, and had dismissed him.

Lippe had left a devastated Germany to teach in Brazil, and from there had gone to Peru to become Head of Research at the company of which he was now the boss. Dramatic events, even by Latin-American standards, had led to his ascent from research lab to executive suite. A boardroom altercation between the chairman and his two top directors had ended in the death of two men and a life sentence for murder for the third.

Dilke sighed and rubbed his eyes.

There was nothing tangible: the mules; the Russian colonel; Lippe's background; mayhem in a South American boardroom. Nothing really connected.

Dilke frowned.

The delayed effects of forty-eight sleepless hours now hit him. He yawned and stretched. There was sand under his eyelids and lead in his arms and legs. He climbed stiffly down the steel ladder, crawled into his bunk and fell asleep instantly.

PART TWO

4

Heathrow was still very dark at seven in the morning. A light fog shrouded the flight-path but Bellamy's plane took off on time, and when he breakfasted high over the English Channel the sky was clear and the pink light of dawn shone in through the cabin window.

When they were half-way across the Atlantic the sun overtook them, and when they called at Antigua and Caracas it blazed in the west.

Dilke was wakened by his wall-clock alarm.

He had slept like a dead man for twenty hours since crawling into his bunk, unconscious of the drive to Heathrow and of the million miles (in micro terms) he had flown since then.

He unzipped the bunk cover then dressed and ate and climbed to the observation chamber. Bellamy was asleep in his seat, his head lolling to one side, his features almost concealed by the swell of his pink jowls. Dilke hardly felt the immense, slow rise and fall of the plane's passage through space. As he strapped himself into his seat the plane's intercom crackled and a metallic voice spoke.

'This is Captain Devas speaking. We are now crossing

the equator, ladies and gentlemen, at four hundred miles per hour, at an altitude of thirty-five thousand feet. Below us is a tributary of the Amazon called the Rio Negro. We will be crossing the Andes mountains in two hours and will arrive in Lima at seventeen hundred hours local time. Thank you, ladies and gentlemen.'

The voice woke Gilbert Bellamy and he looked down sleepily at the meandering threads of water thirty-five thousand feet below as the pilot repeated his message in Spanish.

Mathew Dilke called a good afternoon in Spanish into the Aid mike, and Bellamy blinked down at the tiny flesh-coloured dot which was an upturned face.

As the vast rain-forests unrolled beneath them they crossed more rivers – the Japurá, Putumayo, Marañon – which drain the heartland of the continent, and as they drew nearer to the Andes rain clouds grew thick beneath them, obscuring the land, and crowding against the mountainous barrier.

To the west of the barrier an arid coastal strip lay between the Andes and the Pacific Ocean. The nose of the plane dipped and they began a slow descent towards the sea, a hundred miles away.

Lima was hot and humid.

A glaring heat was reflected from the concrete runway as Bellamy descended from the aircraft, and his forehead was beaded with sweat before he stepped into the airport bus and was whisked away to the terminal buildings; there he left the bus and followed his fellow travellers to the reception hall.

A uniformed chauffeur stood watchfully by the entrance, holding up a small card with C.P.P. printed on it, and as Bellamy caught his eye the man stepped forward and spoke to him. 'Please excuse me, Señor, are you Mister Gilbert Bellamy, the gentleman from London?'

Bellamy mopped his perspiring throat with a handkerchief and gave an affirmative grunt. The man raised the monogrammed card to the glossy peak of his cap in smart salute, asked Bellamy to follow, and led him towards a big white Mercedes which was parked nearby in the shade. As the chauffeur opened the rear door of the car a brown-skinned gold-ringed hand reached out and a voice said, 'Welcome! Welcome to Peru, Mr Bellamy.'

Bellamy shook the hand and joined its owner, a handsome, fleshy man with a thin black moustache, wraparound dark glasses and a thick Portuguese accent – in the air-conditioned interior.

'José! See to the luggage,' the man called, then turned and introduced himself as Cabral, *Emmanuel* Cabral, Sales Manager of Compañía Peruana de Plásticos.

The chauffeur returned quickly with Bellamy's case – passed by customs with a flourish of chalk – and drove out of the airport and into the rush of evening traffic. The citizens of Lima did not submit quietly to the discipline of traffic lights. They drove on their brakes and their horns: squealing to a stop when the lights turned red and blaring at cross-traffic which moved off prematurely.

The Mercedes went east along Lima's main thoroughfare towards a white skyscraper at the centre of the city, and entered the Plaza Fernando de la Fuenté in front of the tall building. Dominating the Plaza was an equestrian statue on a high plinth. GENERAL FERDINAND DE LA FUENTÉ: PRESIDENTÉ DE LA REPUBLICA DEL PERU. The general, in full dress uniform, raised a marble arm in salute and sat very straight on a prancing marble horse. Their appearance of baroque antiquity was an illusion,

43

for the date inscribed on the plinth showed that the general had been president for less than five years.

There was a hooting jam of traffic in the Plaza. As the Mercedes moved in fits and starts Bellamy and Dilke peered up at the skyscraper. It looked less impressive close-up than when seen from afar. Only its lower part was faced with marble, the rest was raw concrete, and its windows were unglazed. A construction crane stood motionless on top and no building activity went on in the fenced-off area at its base.

'Fifty storeys high! Seventy thousand square metres of government office space!' exclaimed Cabral, and Bellamy nodded.

'Completion: mañana!' Dilke said, and Bellamy smiled.

They left the Plaza, entered the older part of the city, and travelled between high buildings and beneath a network of tram-wires and overhead power cables.

The Portuguese leaned forward, 'Turn off to the Plaza Mayor, José.' He turned to Bellamy. 'You must see the cathedral before we leave Lima, Mr Bellamy.'

The cathedral, he explained, was very old and contained the relics of Francisco Pizarro, Spanish founding-father of the state.

They drove through a narrow alley, its bulging plaster walls contained by a thick skin of old bull-fight posters, then passed under an archway into the Plaza.

The cathedral filled one side of the square and José stopped where Bellamy could get a good view of it.

Within the enclosure, the air was oven-hot, and so still that not a leaf moved on the trees which grew around its perimeter. A bony nag in the shafts of a covered landau stood asleep amongst the residual yellow and brown stains from a thousand stand-up nosebag meals.

44

In the centre of the square two children played with a kitten in the dusty bowl of an ornamental fountain. Dust covered the cobbles and coated the shrivelled leaves; the square was full of dust and the smell of dust. An old bent-backed priest sprinkled the cathedral steps with water, then swept the dust down slowly, step-by-step, and across the pavement and into the gutter.

The cathedral was in the Spanish style with massive twin bell-towers and three dark entrances. Its facade was bleached white by the sun, centuries of earth tremors had cracked its walls, and weeds had taken root on its cornices and roof. Three nuns sat on the wall of the dried-up fountain and gazed at the building with impassive Indian faces and ate tortillas out of a brown carrier-bag.

'They keep Pizarro in a glass coffin,' Cabral said. Before Bellamy could respond suitably, he was startled by the sudden appearance of a face outside the window. It was the face of a young boy, who rapped on the glass and smiled ingratiatingly into the car. He ducked down when Cabral waved angrily at him then reappeared with a small girl in his arms, who held up, in turn, a bedraggled kitten.

Cabral spoke to the chauffeur and fished in his pocket for a coin as the electrically-operated window slid down.

With an impudent smile the child thrust the kitten towards Bellamy while her brother called softly and insistently, 'Una sol, Señor. Una sol. Una sol, Señor, una sol.' To Dilke the small creature was a pitiful monster with matted fur and gummed-up eyes, taken too soon from its mother. It twisted feebly in the child's dirty fists and a wretched cry came from its open mouth.

'Una sol!' the children chorused. 'Una sol por el gatillo!'

A huge silvery disc shot into Dilke's view then spun out of the car and bounced across the cobblestones, and as the car slid away from the kerb he saw the two-legged monsters scurry after the coin, dragging the kitten behind them on a length of coarse twine.

They swept out of the Plaza, rejoined the traffic in the avenue and continued their journey towards the blue outline of the Andes in the east.

Desert infiltrated the outskirts of Lima, filling the tramlines with grit and small stones which spat and exploded under the wheels of the trams. At the edge of the city the old avenue changed to a new concrete highway which went flat and straight across the desert towards the mountains.

José put his foot down and the blue flag on the Mercedes' long bonnet became a blur.

A line of dots in the distance changed rapidly into a convoy of big blue trucks carrying rock towards Lima and the coast.

Half-way to the foothills a side road joined the highway. A truck with a faded C.P.P. monogram on its cab door rattled along it and lurched without pause or warning on to the highway ahead of the Mercedes. José gave a prolonged blast on the horn as he swung out to avoid collision and Dilke saw a packed truckload of swaying figures; heard the crash and groan of changing gears, and glimpsed the truck-driver's impassive brown face as they passed.

'Christ damn all Indians,' Cabral sighed.

Now the highway divided into two; disappearing into scrub on the left and curving to the right towards a distant cluster of tall, white, tree-shaded buildings. 'The Residence of the Presidenté de la Republica!'

The words rolled off Cabral's tongue; the Mercedes

took the left fork; the palace vanished behind roadside bushes, and the first foothill rose before them and obscured the Andes.

The road switch-backed smoothly over a series of ridges then entered a landscape of high hills with domed summits and steep sides like enormous inverted pudding basins.

After twenty kilometres of hill road they rounded a bend and came suddenly on an old Indian woman driving a small herd of llamas along the roadside. The beasts panicked as José gave a warning blast on his horn, and as the car swept by Dilke saw them scatter and scramble up the rocky hillside.

Cabral looked back through the rear window and mimicked the old woman's rapidly fading cries in a shaky falsetto. He was still laughing when they came in sight of a hangar-like building at the foot of a hill with COMPAÑÍA PERUANA DE PLÁSTICOS faintly visible on its curved side under a coating of grey dust.

The hill was a huge truncated cone, bigger than the domed hills which surrounded it, with a road cut into its steep side leading to a building on its summit.

They turned off the main highway, passed the factory and drove up the hill. Cabral was promising cocktails before dinner and a view of unsurpassed splendour from the hilltop when Dilke spoke quietly into his mike: 'Gilbert. Mules.'

They flashed past the animals in seconds but Bellamy had time to see a mule in a small stockade by the roadside, separated by the high fence from a dozen others which stood with heads hanging, tails whisking and belly skins twitching at the onslaught of blood-sucking insects.

They had two fleeting glimpses of the factory and the dust-covered lower slopes as they swept up the steep road which encircled the hill twice before levelling out just short of the hilltop.

Seen from the valley the C.P.P. headquarters had seemed small against the massive scale of the landscape. Now it loomed at the end of the road like a space-age castle of concrete and glass, set into the rock and jutting out over the precipitous hillside on huge cantilevered beams.

José swung the Mercedes into a gap between the cars parked beneath the overhanging building and Bellamy stepped out and stretched and breathed in deeply.

'Pure mountain air, Mr Bellamy! Up here our laboratories are entirely free of dust and contamination.'

The evening sun was hot, but after the humidity on the coast the air was fresh and cool. Bellamy smiled and took in another lungful, then followed the Portuguese towards the entrance to the building.

Access to the fortress-like headquarters of Peruana de Plásticos was by massive goods-elevator or by a small passenger-elevator.

Cabral waved to a uniformed guard in a glass booth as he ushered Bellamy into the elevator which took them smoothly to the top floor of the building.

They walked down a thickly carpeted corridor – lined with numbered doors, like the bedrooms in a small private hotel – and entered a big, sunlit, flamboyant room with jungle-green curtains, a huge banana-yellow sofa and a cream-coloured carpet.

Wide windows gave Bellamy his promised, unsurpassed view of the Peruvian scene. Beyond the bizarre pudding-basin landscape, through which they had just travelled, Lima shimmered on the horizon where desert merged with sea.

Bellamy complimented Cabral on the view then sank into the bulging sofa and sipped the triple pink gin his host had mixed at the technicoloured bar.

Between more gins and the commencement of dinner Bellamy was shown his bedroom. 'Our friends find it more convenient to stay here than in a Lima hotel. And it saves time,' Cabral explained.

'Keep to general chat as much as you can, Gilbert,' Dilke said. 'The longer you put off business the longer I have to look around.'

But before dinner, while Cabral and Bellamy stood together, looking across hills which were now humped black shadows rimmed with red, and watching a sunset like the last act of *Götterdämmerung*, Cabral began his sales talk.

'The wealth of this company lies in those hills,' he turned solemnly to Bellamy, 'and in the genius of Professor Heinrich Lippe.'

'This is earthquake country. All the way down Peru there is a weakness in the crust of the earth through which volcanoes have erupted for millions of years.' He extended an arm. 'Millions of years ago those hills were active volcanoes.' He pointed to the floor. 'We stand on the rim of an extinct volcano at this moment, Mr Bellamy!'

The building had been erected there by the professor – Cabral went on – when he became chairman and managing director, and had revolutionized the plastics industry by using volcanic minerals as basic material.

'Tomorrow all this will be made clear, Mr Bellamy. I have made a film which you must see, and we will visit the laboratories and the factory.'

Cabral showed the film in the executive conference-room

next morning: half an hour of plodding industrial photography followed an epic shot of erupting lava and the sound of massed drums and cymbals.

'Superb! I would like to borrow that to show to my colleagues in London, Mr Cabral,' Bellamy cried. He showed equal enthusiasm for a display of plastic goods which illustrated the versatility of Heinrich Lippe's production techniques; picking up a simulated-leather briefcase (a *fraction* of the cost of real leather, Mr Bellamy), a jet-engine rotor blade (*indestructible*, Mr Bellamy), and a lightweight steel-bonded-to-plastic radiator grille (it *looks* like solid steel but the metal is only paper-thin!).

'And now I must meet your professor, Mr Cabral, and see where all these exciting technical developments take place.'

'Of course! We will go to the laboratories now. Unfortunately Professor Lippe is engaged on research at the moment,' Cabral smiled regretfully. 'But the head of our laboratories will be glad to see you.'

It was time to start work. Dilke settled himself in his seat and checked his camera. Now he would record anything and everything which might give a clue to Lippe's activities.

They descended to the lower floor and entered a small laboratory which contained an electron microscope on a meticulously tidy work-bench, a high stool, racks of chemicals and a staff holiday-chart pinned to a wall. The room was unoccupied. Dilke set his zoom-lens at wide-angle and began to shoot. Cabral stood hesitantly for a moment then said, 'He may be with the professor; they may know in the main laboratory,' and left the room.

Bellamy watched him pass along the corridor (his

figure distorted by the frosted-glass partition wall) and listened to the fading sound of his footsteps.

A door in a small cupboard above the bench was open a crack. Bellamy opened it with a finger; inside was a row of square-backed folders. Bellamy took two quick steps and silently closed the door to the room then took out a folder and opened it on the bench-top. And Dilke photographed it.

There were written and typed and printed pages. There was no time to read them, only time to record them. They had rehearsed the procedure. Turn page, and click shutter. Bellamy kept one eye on the wall of frosted glass and listened for footsteps as he flicked the pages over.

Turn, click. Turn, click.

'Faster, Gilbert!'

Turn, click, turn, click, turn, click.

They had almost finished three folders when they heard Cabral's voice.

Bellamy shut the folder, replaced it, closed the cupboard and leaned back against the bench with folded arms as the Portuguese came bustling in, followed by a man in a laboratory coat.

Cabral introduced Herr Schmidt, head of chemical research and deputy to Professor Lippe.

Schmidt was a tall, gaunt German who displayed little sign of pleasure at his visitor's presence: after giving Bellamy the stiff courtesy of a minimal bow from the hips, he stood in silence with his hands deep in his overall pockets.

Dilke photographed him.

He would not be difficult to identify if he was in the Ministry files. The chemist had bony features, a narrow head, and only one eye. From behind an opaque circle of glass in his metal-framed spectacles blazed the relic of an old laboratory accident. A ragged star of dead, white flesh was burnt into his sallow skin. As the German bent over the big microscope, inserting slides of different plastic structures, Dilke had a close-up view of his scarred face. Acid had splashed the ear, shrivelling cartilage and lobe, and spurted down his cheek and jaw, leaving a track of granulated flesh like the surface of a dead planet.

Schmidt gave concise, monosyllabic answers to Bellamy's questions but Bellamy was unable to direct the talk towards non-technical subjects and his attempt to discover something of the German's background and experience was unsuccessful. 'Leave it, Gilbert. You can pump Cabral about Schmidt later on.'

The main labs were cool, interconnected rooms shaded from the tropical sun by slatted blinds, and the laboratory staff bent silently over their work as Bellamy was shown round.

The knowledge of plastics which Gilbert Bellamy had gained during his tour of the laboratories in Kent enabled him to discuss the subject with some show of expertise, and he stopped to talk to each technician (who smiled nervously under the cold eye of Schmidt) about his work. They were all Peruvians who spoke imperfect English, and Bellamy prolonged his talks with them (to give Dilke time to photograph every flask, bottle and piece of equipment in sight) by concealing his knowledge of Spanish.

Bellamy extended his visit to the laboratories so successfully that Cabral put off the factory visit to the following day and took him out to the nearest quarry after lunch.

The grand concrete highway ended abruptly a short distance beyond the factory and a number of dirt roads fanned out from it and disappeared into winding valleys between the great hills.

One of the tracks brought them to a quarry which was half-excavated.

It was a stunning introduction to the source of Compañía Peruana de Plásticos' raw materials.

Half of the great domed hill had been blasted and cut away revealing the strata of the dead volcano. A solidified fountain of different coloured lava gushed out from its central core. Coloured band lay upon coloured band, just as they had flowed up out of the earth millions of years before. Red, brown, ochre, orange and grey; a colour-coded mass of different chemical and mineral deposits which, when replasticized by Heinrich Lippe's twentieth-century alchemy, would be transformed into the tools and kitchenware and knick-knacks of the modern world.

As they watched masses of rock being dynamited off the face of the hill and loaded into trucks by gangs of labourers, Cabral talked about a specific business deal for the first time since Bellamy's arrival. He offered, as a package deal, manufacturing secrets, patent rights, and raw material shipped to anywhere in the world. He waved a hand at the vista of unbreached volcanic hills which stretched for as far as the eye could see: the material was not only unique but the supply was virtually limitless.

Dilke sat strapped into his seat, impatiently listening to the charade in which the Portuguese was an unwitting actor, and shaken by the noise and vibration from the huge trucks which groaned up from the floor of the quarry and roared off towards the highway, trailing billowing clouds of coloured dust.

* * *

The factory was an aircraft hangar which the Republic had generously supplied to Compañía Peruana de Plásticos in the interests of the national economy, Cabral explained. ('In which the president has shares according to my files,' Dilke said). The temperature beneath its sheet metal arc was in the nineties when Bellamy did his tour.

Apart from the heat and dirt the factory was much the same as the English one. The same German machines churned out the same yellow buckets, watched in the same lack-lustre way by somnambulist machine-minders.

By the time they reached the fibreglass bonding section Bellamy had had enough. Teams of Indians were smoothing boat-hulls with electric sanders and the air was thick with flying plastic and glass fibre.

Gilbert Bellamy sneezed convulsively.

Dilke saw the glint of powdered glass particles falling past the observation dome.

'I think I've seen enough. I need a breath of fresh air, Mr Cabral,' Bellamy wheezed. '*How* do those men work without masks?'

'Ah! Mr Bellamy. They are accustomed to it; they would not use masks if they had them.'

Bellamy brushed dust from his jacket and sneezed again, and Dilke spoke urgently into the mike: 'We are getting nowhere. You must meet Lippe. I must have a chance to investigate his office.'

Cabral glanced at his watch as they left the bonding section. 'We will return to the office, Mr Bellamy. There you can have a shower and a drink before lunch. We can return to the factory when it is cooler.'

'An excellent plan, Mr Cabral! And perhaps I can see Professor Lippe in the meantime.' The words had an emphasis which made them rather more than a request. 'I have heard so much about the professor that I would be *very* sorry to leave without seeing him,' Bellamy said firmly.

Cabral sighed. 'The problem is, Mr Bellamy, that Professor Lippe is always so preoccupied with his researches that he rarely sees visitors ...'

Bellamy looked at him silently.

'To be absolutely frank, Mr Bellamy, I seldom have the opportunity to see the professor myself ...'

Bellamy's expression was suddenly very cold.

'I will telephone him when we get back,' Cabral said quickly, 'and see what I can arrange.'

Bellamy was dressing after his shower when the Portuguese came to his room with the news that Professor Lippe was free to see him during the afternoon.

At lunchtime Cabral ate rather less and drank rather more than he had on the previous day, and the suppressed triumph with which he had given the news that the professor would see them faded as the meal progressed.

When they had finished lunch, and Bellamy sat contentedly on the sofa turning the pages of a lavishly illustrated coffee-table book on the ancient and ruined city of Cuzco, Cabral stood at the window and gazed through it in an abstracted way.

They were to see Lippe at two-thirty. Cabral checked his watch with increasing frequency as the time approached, and at twenty-nine minutes past two he led Bellamy from the room. They passed the guest rooms and the conference room, and came to a white door at the end of a long corridor. The carpet ended at the door; the floor of the corridor beyond it was smooth, black and shiny. Cabral stopped at a door on the left and knocked lightly on it. He paused and listened and knocked again, then he opened the door hesitantly and looked in.

5

Professor Heinrich Lippe's room on the top floor of his concrete and glass headquarters was level with the rim of the dead volcano and overlooked a lake which filled its crater.

Gilbert Bellamy stood in the entrance to the room and saw a breathtaking panorama of the Peruvian Andes through a wall of tinted glass which formed the eastern side of the room.

The room was study, workshop and library combined; forty feet by thirty feet; with a huge, black, Gothic desk standing in the middle of it.

The glare of light on the terrace outside was transmuted into an aquatic green by the tinted glass. Nothing moved but a screenful of dancing white dots on a television near the desk, and sluggish serpents of sunlight reflected on to the ceiling from the surface of the lake.

There was perfect silence; then Bellamy heard a soft repeated cough and a man rose from a high-backed chair behind the desk.

Professor Lippe had the sprawling and engaging ugliness of an old orang-utan; with a beige face blotched

with freckles, small brown eyes set in pouches of dis-
coloured skin, fine white hair sticking out in all directions, and tufted white eyebrows raised in perpetual –
and somehow clownish – inquiry.

He was dressed in a blue bush-shirt with short sleeves,
and blue linen slacks – both garments were faded and
crumpled – and wore rope-soled canvas sneakers which
creaked gently as he slowly approached Bellamy across
the polished, black floor.

'Good afternoon, Mr Bellamy. I am most happy to
meet you. I hope that you are enjoying your visit to
Peru.' His English was excellent, with hardly a trace of
accent. He spoke slowly and distinctly in a low, hoarse
voice, pausing for a wheezing intake of breath between
each sentence. The hand which he extended to Bellamy
was moist and warm and Bellamy could feel the bones
beneath the loose skin.

'Mr Cabral and I have had some very interesting talks,
Professor, and he has shown me a great deal since I
arrived here . . .'

'Cabral must not press you too hard, Mr Bellamy.
Selling plastics is his obsession.' Lippe revealed a row
of china-white dentures and his sales manager gave a
nervous answering smile.

The old man gently touched Bellamy's arm, took him
across the room to the huge window and looked for a
long minute at the great mountains and cloudless sky,
and their reflections in the lake. 'No part of the world
exceeds the grandeur of Peru, Mr Bellamy. You must see
something of its beauties while you are here, as well as
its more material aspects.'

There was a click and Schmidt stepped through a door
in the wall, carrying a clip-board under his arm and a
jar of yellow crystals.

'Not now, Schmidt!' Lippe said, and the gaunt German turned and disappeared again. The door was covered with the same material as the surrounding wall and was barely discernible. Dilke stared at it thoughtfully; the only trace of the man's brief presence in the room were powdery foot-marks on the black floor, and a faint and slightly sickly smell which entered the ventilation slits in the observation dome and which he could not identify.

The old man returned unperturbed to the virtues of Peru. 'If you are interested in history, Mr Bellamy, you should visit some of the cities which were built here before the arrival of the Spanish. They are relics of the most advanced civilization in the Americas and contain sculpture and pottery which were never excelled by the civilizations of the old world.'

The professor led Bellamy to the end of the room where pictures hung and a large ceramic pot stood on a painted wooden stand. He brushed the side of the pot with his fingertips and it spun slowly on a concealed turntable.

'This is a Peruvian urn, Mr Bellamy, which was discovered on the site of this building.' A telephone on his desk rang and he left, with an apology, to answer it. Cabral, who had followed them mutely since entering the room, took up the theme animatedly: 'It is a very old Inca pot; in it they put the hearts of sacrificed Indians! Its value is incalculable.'

The professor's voice was a faint whisper of sound in the distance. Cabral showed Bellamy pictures and a case of terracotta figurines, then with a glance towards the high-backed chair which concealed its occupant, he took Bellamy through a glass door in the glass wall to show him a statue on the terrace.

It was a dazzling, white, life-sized sculpture of a horse standing with its legs spread and its head outstretched.

'It is sprayed with plastic,' Cabral said, and added with enthusiasm, 'The whole terrace has been sprayed also, making it impervious to all extremes of temperature and climatic conditions.'

'I am afraid my sales manager is a philistine, Mr Bellamy!' The professor stood smiling behind them, sheltered from the sun by a white silk umbrella, yellowed with age. He went to the statue, and touched its rough flank and the smooth curve of its jaw.

'Is he not a splendid creature? Combining the formality of your Barbara Hepworth and the romanticism of the surrealists. Will you guess who created him, Mr Bellamy? Giacometti perhaps? Marini?'

Bellamy smiled placidly. 'I'm afraid I too am a philistine when it comes to modern art, Professor Lippe.'

'Ah!' the old man sighed regretfully, 'but you are, no doubt, not impervious to the beauty of natural things.'

He folded his umbrella and gave a breathless whistle; a flash of iridescent colour appeared from nowhere and hovered in the air above him. He took from his pocket a small bottle with a little spout on it and held it up, and the tiny ball of flame flew down and inserted a needle-thin beak into the spout. It was a humming-bird no bigger than a bumble bee. More of the tiny birds appeared to take their turns at the feeding-bottle. 'I import them from Cuba, Mr Bellamy. Though they are nectar sippers they do not despise my humble sugar-water, as you see.' With a gentle flourish of his hand he dispersed the birds, then he pocketed the bottle, raised his silk umbrella again and walked to the terrace wall.

The lake was a perfect circle a hundred yards across; green lily leaves floated at its centre, and it was surrounded by lush tropical vegetation (quite unlike the stunted scrub which grew on the hillsides) which drew moisture from the soil on the volcano's rim. The terrace wall sloped out into the lake and joined a curved underwater shelf several yards wide which overhung the deep water-filled crater. Terrace, parapet and underwater shelf were all covered with the same skin of snow-white plastic. A smell of hot plastic filled Mathew Dilke's nostrils, and he saw fish lying in the green water which covered the shelf as Bellamy leaned over the parapet.

A steel tray, filled with finely minced meat, rested on the low parapet wall. 'First my birds and now my fish. Your visit has coincided with feeding time, Mr Bellamy.' Professor Lippe smiled, and dexterously emptied the tray into the water. The swish of its contents hitting the surface attracted more fish and soon a small shoal of them were feeding indolently on the shelf bottom.

A scent of tobacco drifted into the viewing chamber and Dilke looked towards Cabral and the professor.

The Portuguese held the white umbrella over the old man as he filled a pipe from an oilskin pouch. The professor's eyes were not on his pipe, nor on the fish, but were studying Bellamy's profile, and the expression on his face seemed suddenly less benign than before. As the blunt fingers held a match to the tobacco, Dilke detected a cold glint in the eyes which stared through the rising smoke, but the voice which spoke between slow puffs on the pipe was amiable enough. 'My fish pond is practical as well as decorative, Mr Bellamy. It supplies water to the factory. It fills up in the rainy season, and its level is sustained during the summer with water pumped up from underground springs.'

Gilbert Bellamy made an appreciative noise in his throat and took out a handkerchief and mopped his brow. The heat was intolerable. Lippe dropped the match over the edge of the parapet, reclaimed his umbrella and led the way back to the coolness of his room where he soon, courteously but firmly, said goodbye.

Cabral and Bellamy did not return to the factory but stayed at headquarters for the rest of the afternoon and discussed business.

Dilke sat in his dome, only half-aware of their talk, and reviewed all that he had seen and heard since arriving in Peru. It did not amount to much; but he could draw one conclusion: unless a laboratory was hidden away in the hills or the factory, which seemed very unlikely, any illicit research must be taking place in the headquarters building somewhere. Yet Bellamy's tour of the laboratories had revealed nothing, none of the equipment resembled the equipment at Porton. And there had been neither sight, sound nor smell of a mule.

But – the thought came suddenly – the rock which surrounded the building could be honeycombed with stables and labs ... there could be miles of galleries in the rock ... the steel goods-elevator was big enough to carry a dozen mules at a time ...

He was going too damned fast! Dreaming up phantom rock-caves before the building itself was properly investigated. And a lab need not be all that big. Not as big as Porton, which was equipped to manufacture germ weapons as well as research them, and, being government-owned, had probably obeyed a bricks-and-mortar Parkinson's law anyway.

It was time for him to separate from Bellamy. He would start in Lippe's room, which was only a few micro-miles away from Bellamy's bedroom, along corridor skirting boards for most of the way. It was the logical place to start: the centre of power within the organization. Dilke remembered the German chemist's entry into the room and the professor's dismissal of him, and he felt a sharp interest in what lay behind the door through which the German had disappeared.

Cabral pushed away the papers which covered the low table and pocketed the pen with which he had been scribbling long columns of figures.

'Enough for today, Mr Bellamy! Tonight we will drive into Lima and we will dine at my club, and we shall relax and see some night life. What do you say to that, Mr Bellamy?'

Bellamy sat back beaming on the yellow sofa and thought it was a splendid idea. He went to his room to freshen up; hung his jacket on a chair-back, then washed and shaved and changed his shirt.

Dilke watched him select a tie, then he depressed the volume-booster lever on the arm of his chair.

'How long can you stall Cabral, Gilbert?'

Bellamy stood before the wardrobe mirror and carefully knotted his tie.

'Oh. I can haggle for a while yet. There are a dozen permutations on the deal he is offering, and I still haven't concluded my factory visit. What progress have we made? I've spotted nothing significant myself.'

'Nor have I. But tonight's jaunt might lead somewhere. A boozed-up Cabral might let something slip if he's steered in the right direction.'

Cabral was mixing drinks when Bellamy rejoined him. He had cleared away the business papers which had littered the low table and the floor, and the book about Cuzco which Bellamy had browsed through after lunch was back on the table. An equally thick and expensively produced volume lay beside it. The book was called *Samantha*. Just one word, printed white on glossy black in elegant Bodoni capitals, with the lipsticked imprint of a kiss reproduced beneath it. The book contained, as Bellamy discovered when he opened it, exquisite pictures of the world's finest cities. Samantha appeared in each picture. The first photograph, all blues and pearly greys, showed her copulating serenely on the flat roof of a skyscraper in the milky light of dawn, with the silhouette of a phallic Chrysler Building in the background. It was de-luxe pornography.

Subsequent pictures showed her taking part in a wide variety of sexual couplings, and satisfying the erotic appetites of a multi-racial clientele. Dilke detected a slight check in the rhythm of his partner's breathing when he opened the book, then Bellamy turned each page and examined each new revelation with aplomb.

A glossy Polaroid snapshot fell out from between the last two pages, and as Bellamy picked it up Dilke saw Cabral at the bar with a half-smile on his lips, watching his guest from the corner of his eyes.

The Polaroid shot lacked the artistry of Samantha's pictures. Two naked women sat grinning on a yellow sofa; a blonde and a brunette, with their legs crossed and with glasses in their hands. As Cabral placed drinks on the table Bellamy returned the picture, closed the book and picked up his gin with a bland smile.

After a second drink they descended to the car park where Cabral dismissed his driver. The Portuguese drove very fast – having arranged to meet some friends, he explained – overtaking trucks with sustained fanfares on the horn and reaching Lima in little over the half-hour.

LA CLUB AMERICANA shone in bright neon blue over the club entrance, but the crossed neon flags of Peru and America were switched off in recognition of the discord between the two countries.

Cabral left the car at the kerb, tossed the keys to the man at the door, and took Gilbert Bellamy across thick carpets, through gilded doors and into the plush club bar.

Cabral's friends were called Gladys and Dolores. Blonde and brunette; American, and Spanish with a dash of Indian; Gladys chain-smoked Chesterfields and drank straight rye, and Dolores, who had beautiful eyes, perfect teeth and a bold Peruvian nose, drank Bacardi and Coke and chewed gum in a daintily lady-like way.

The fourway conversation which followed Bellamy's introduction to the girls (complicated by Dolores's imperfect English and Bellamy's need to continue his pretence that he knew no Spanish) put paid to Dilke's idea that Bellamy could gently lead Cabral along paths of indiscretion into fields of revelation.

All that Dilke learned during the evening, as they moved from the cocktail bar to supper table and back to the bar again, was the depressingly negative fact that the Portuguese had been with Compañía Peruana de Plásticos for only a short time and was probably not worth much as a source of undercover information.

At eleven, during the course of a strident floor-show, Cabral decided that they would continue the evening in quieter, more intimate surroundings. At his suite back at C.P.P. there were drinks ... soft lights ... sweet music ... Cabral winked: perhaps a little private filmshow ...

Bellamy excused himself and went to the cloakroom and through a door marked *Caballeros*; he passed an attendant in a white jacket who was polishing wash-basin taps, walked to the last of a long row of urinals and stepped up close to the high-level bowl.

Dilke heard the sound of a fly-zip, like the rattle of a greased chain running through a steel hatch, and the first whisper of Bellamy's water on the side of the bowl.

Bellamy spoke in an undertone, 'Mathew. I'm afraid we've got nothing out of the evening *information-wise*,' he gave the last words a wry American stress, 'and unless you can think of a new ploy I can't see things getting better.'

A great jet of urine shot out beyond and below the curve of Bellamy's paunch, hit a target of concentric circles which was engraved on the back of the urinal, and flooded down to create a turbulent whirlpool in the porcelain bowl.

'Information-wise it's been a bloody disaster. We've lost time, Gilbert. You may have to extend your stay somehow.'

The jet of liquid lost its force and slowly fell away to thunder into the bowl then disappear from sight behind the curve of the great belly.

'Take a trip up to Cuzco and take a look at Lippe's Inca civilization; you can tell Cabral you need a break to think things over; I can ferret about while you're away.'

A spasm went through Bellamy's body and Dilke saw a last spurt, milky with sediment, hit the frothing surface far below. 'Gravel!' Bellamy muttered. 'Must see the quack.' A torrent of clear water flushed down, sweeping the golden liquid and the cloudy sediment through the perforated trap which covered the waste-pipe. Bellamy dipped gently at the knees and Dilke heard the stutter of the closing zip.

65

'Just carry on for the rest of the night, Gilbert. Keep Cabral talking; he may just let something drop which will give us a lead. Get him talking about Lippe and about Schmidt if you can.'

Bellamy heard Dilke's voice faintly through the squirt and bubble of water from all down the line of gleaming stalls, and nodded his great head.

6

They left the tramlines and neon lights of the city behind and travelled inland along the broad dual-carriageway.

The night was black.

The road, blinding white in the headlights, lay as straight as a lance for fifty kilometres. A scattered pattern of lights to the south, like those of a small township, marked the residence of President Fernando de la Fuenté.

The highway forked to right and left; they took the factory road into the foothills, the Mercedes diving and swooping along its wide curves. Cabral drove with Gladys at his side, and Bellamy sat behind with Dolores. The Portuguese steered with one languid hand on the wheel and a cigar in the other. Drifting cigar smoke, visible in the light from the car radio, hung momentarily near the open quarter light before being sucked out into the car's slipstream.

Dilke sat in the Aid's viewing chamber and watched the whiplash of smoke flash past the car window. As Bellamy had got nothing out of Cabral during the evening it was time for him to leave base and start his reconnaissance.

A booming samba from the radio filled the car. Cabral turned his head and leered over his shoulder at the brunette; his lips moved but the samba drowned the words.

Dilke looked up at Bellamy. His companion's huge head lay back against the upholstery, the features concealed by the swelling curve of his great jowl. Dilke spoke into the intercom but no movement of any kind showed that Bellamy had heard. Dilke turned up the volume.

'Gilbert!' Tonight I will check the room leading from Lippe's office. Stick the pin in the skirting-board near your bedroom door.'

Bellamy's chin swung down; the glowing end of a cigar butt came into view, followed by pursed lips then the black caverns of his nostrils and half-closed eyes. A corner of his mouth lifted in a smile and an eyelid slid down in a ponderous wink.

Dolores' eyes were on Bellamy's face.

The steady rotation of her jaw slowly came to a stop. Dilke saw her mouth twist into a licentious and compliant smile.

The lips parted. A glistening block of gum appeared on the tip of her massive tongue; it was transported between the great teeth and taken by a finger and thumb; a hauser of saliva joining tongue to chewing gum broke as the hand moved away and sank into darkness under the edge of the seat. Leaning her body closer to Bellamy, the girl slid her arm through his.

The observation dome filled with the smell of brandy and cigars, mingled with the smell of spearmint; heavy perfume floated from the moist valley between the girl's breasts. Perspiration greased the pouched flesh beneath Bellamy's eyes and gleamed on his upper lip.

Dilke curled his nostrils. Part two of the evening's entertainment! The heavy breathing bit.

A white Mercedes – twin to their own – overtook them on the crest of a hill and dropped neatly in front of them two car lengths away.

What followed happened with startling speed.

Brake-lights glowed ahead and, suddenly, the Portuguese had both hands on the wheel; Dilke felt a rapid deceleration. The reversing light on the front car blazed twice; Cabral crushed his cigar in an ashtray and leaned forward tensely. A winking red light signalled a left turn; they swung off the highway after the car and followed it along a dirt road for a score of yards. Both cars stopped.

Cabral stepped out hesitantly and stood half-in and half-out of the car.

A man walked towards them with a hand raised against the glare of their headlights. It was Schmidt. Dilke saw two discs of reflected light flash from the shadow beneath the hand then the tall figure was obscured by Cabral's body.

The radio drowned their words, but Cabral's gestures expressed confusion then resentment and finally, with an angry shrug, ill-tempered assent. He leaned in and snapped nervously at his blonde, who poked at three buttons before she got the one which stopped the Latin beat.

When he pulled open Gilbert Bellamy's door he had adjusted his features to show sincere regret.

'Mr Bellamy. I am most terribly sorry! There is an emergency. I must immediately return to Lima. I did not know of this before, but I must meet people on the night plane.' Cabral opened the door to its full extent. 'But Herr Schmidt will take you on in his car.'

Obedient to the implicit request, Bellamy left the yielding comfort of his seat with a sigh and got out.

Cabral shut the door, stepped smartly round to his own seat and drove off. A shower of loose stones flew from the spinning wheels, the car rocked up an incline and slewed round on to the road to Lima. The gears went smoothly through a series of fading arpeggios and the sound of the engine died to nothing.

A smell of dung filled the air.

Bellamy turned and stared around in a dazed way. He was beside a roughly fenced pig-pen beyond which shacks, roofed with flattened petrol drums, crowded a hillside.

An inquiring grunt came from a shelter within the pen and a strident continuation of the samba which had filled the car came faintly from a shack on the hill.

The air was very still, and felt cold after the over-heated car. Bellamy shivered and looked with displeasure at Schmidt.

As he stepped towards the waiting Mercedes its reversing lights came on, lighting the scene with dazzling clarity. A squat figure in a linen suit got out of the car and moved forward with a fat swagger. Bellamy saw that the man was hatless, shoeless and wore no shirt beneath his jacket. The garments were ill-matched: the trousers too short and tight, and the jacket sleeves too long, their cuffs turned back over thick forearms. Both the man and his clothes were repulsively dirty.

Bellamy turned uneasily towards the silent chemist.

'What is this, Herr Schmidt?'

Schmidt gave no reply.

A young pig crawled from the shelter and sniffed the air. It was joined by the rest of the litter which conversed in grunts then trotted to the fence.

Bellamy's eyes blinked rapidly behind thick lenses; he spoke again, his voice sharp with exasperation and rising alarm. 'Look here, Schmidt! What the hell is going on?'

Schmidt's bony face was expressionless, he stood stiffly, his arms at his sides. A dull gleam of light from his right hand caught Bellamy's eye. The muzzle of a gun showed below the closed fist, its short barrel half concealed in a fold of his grey trousers. Schmidt reached out, twitched Bellamy's spectacles from his face and flicked them over the fence. Bellamy stumbled back, swore explosively and incoherently, and tried desperately to focus his blurred vision. Two dark shapes moved between him and the light.

No threat had been spoken, no hand had touched him but Bellamy felt a dreadful premonition, a quailing of the flesh. His body was taken by a spasm of shivering.

Behind him, the pigs squealed peevishly for food.

Shaken by his companion's agitation Dilke grabbed at the seat arms and glared through the transparent wall.

The man in the lightweight suit stood very close, his head level with Dilke, his eyes fixed intently on Bellamy's face. He was lit from behind, but enough light was reflected from Bellamy's shirt-front to illuminate a notably brutal and debauched face. It was a fat, expressionless, yellow-brown face with a ragged fringe of black hair adhering damply to the forehead and the hairs of a sparse moustache sprouting over greasy lips. As Dilke watched, a barely perceptible smile curled the lips.

Dilke looked up quickly through the dome. Bellamy's great fists kneaded and dug at his eyes, then he averted his face from the glaring spotlight leaving only his profile visible. Dilke saw a corner of the mouth; a nostril; a rolling eye. The inflamed eyelids blinked again and again then squeezed tight shut; fluid oozed between the closed lids and spilled down the great curve of the cheek.

Dilke dropped his eyes. The man had moved. His smile had become a scowl.

He had shifted his stance, his right shoulder had swung forward and Dilke saw his jacket come open. Dilke stiffened. Only the great head and shoulders were visible from his seat.

Dilke threw off his harness and leapt forward. In the shadows below, a hand drew back the jacket and revealed the hilt of a knife. There was a dreamlike slowness about the man's movements; Dilke saw light gleam on the copper wire which bound the knife-handle and saw a thick hand slide it from its black leather sheath. The man spread his legs, pivoted his solid torso to the right and drew back his arm.

Dilke struck the perspex with his flat hands and yelled with all the strength of his lungs.

'Gilbert! A knife!'

Shout, knife-thrust, and Bellamy's response were split seconds apart.

As Bellamy punched out blindly the knife flashed towards him. As his wild blow struck his assailant's chest the blade entered Bellamy's body. As the thug fell back the knife was ripped out again.

A long, long, piercing scream shocked the pigs into silence and sent them scrambling for shelter.

Schmidt reached out and plucked at the hearing-aid flex, jerking the transporter from Bellamy's pocket: gravitational pressure brought Dilke to his knees.

The transporter spun at the end of its cable: centrifugal force flattened Dilke against the perspex wall; blurred faces flashed past his eyes. In a series of frozen images, like slowed-down movie shots, Dilke saw Bellamy fall back against the fence; saw his white shirt turn red; saw Bellamy's bloody hands holding his great ruptured belly.

The spinning transporter slowed to a stop. In the long moment before it began its reverse spin Dilke saw the man with the knife crouch, grab Bellamy's legs and, with savage energy, up-end him over the fence into the reeking mud, Schmidt twirled the cord of the hearing aid around his forefinger, caught earplug and container in mid-air and dropped them into his side pocket.

Dilke was thrown from end to end of his observation chamber and blacked out.

Dilke lay on his back and listened to voices; men's voices which seemed to come from far away.

His head throbbed. He opened his eyes and found that he lay in a transparent bowl with light filtering through a huge mesh of coarse fibres illuminating a tangle of cables and big metal shapes outside the bowl. The lights and the strange shapes shifted all around him and he smelt an acrid oily smell.

He shut his eyes and groaned.

There were two voices: a soft, slow, questioning voice, and a voice which gave clipped answers.

'For a businessman he had a very long nose, eh, Schmidt? And for a deaf man he had very sharp ears!'

'Yes, Herr Professor.'

'Where is he now?'

'I left him near the road to Lima thirty minutes ago.'

Dilke opened his eyes wide and stared up. Upside-down on the floor above was his viewing chair. For a moment he was totally disorientated, then he realized that he was lying in the transparent dome of the Aid, and that the Aid was upside down. He strained his ears.

'How did he die?' the soft voice whispered.

'He was killed with a knife, Professor. I employed a professional.'

'And there were no witnesses?'

'No, Herr Professor. I sent away Cabral and two women before the killing.'

'Then they will connect you with the killing in their minds, and you will be implicated when the body is found.'

'Cabral will do as I instruct him. I have spoken on the telephone to him in Lima. He will report to the police that the Englishman was taken from his car by hooded men. Money and threats will silence the women.'

'Good, Schmidt. That is good. It will pass for a bungled kidnapping.'

Dilke heard a sigh of contentment, then the soft voice continued, 'If there are any complications inform me at once; I can speak to the general if it becomes necessary. Tomorrow I will speak to the British Embassy and convey my regrets. The assassin: has he been paid?'

'No, Herr Professor. Not yet.'

'I would like to see him and speak to him and reward him myself.'

'I will send him to you in the morning.'

Dilke felt a turbulent movement. The Aid rose rapidly upwards. He heard the scraping of fibres and the grating of metal against the outside of the dome then light suddenly blazed in his eyes.

Schmidt held the Aid in one hand and a gun in the other. Through the perspex Dilke saw his giant finger disentangle the earplug cable from the trigger-guard (the smell Dilke had smelt had been gun oil and stale cordite fumes); then the chemist returned the gun to his jacket pocket and stood the Aid on the professor's desk.

Dilke fell out of the dome and crashed to the floor of the chamber.

A desk lamp shone above him and he saw the shadowy figure of Heinrich Lippe sitting back in his great winged chair smoking his pipe and looking down at the Aid.

'Ah! You brought the mysterious deaf aid.' Outside the pocket the voice sounded harsher and louder. 'That is good. What do you suppose this gadget is? Some sort of transmitter or radiophone? Take it Schmidt. Examine it tomorrow and tell me what you find.'

Lippe reached out and picked up the Aid. The floor tilted sharply beneath Dilke, he slid down the slope, crashed violently into the chair and grabbed at its foot-bar to stop his fall.

Lippe's huge hand suddenly stopped half-way to his assistant's extended palm.

The Aid tilted even more until Dilke was left swinging from the bar, hanging on with both hands.

He heard a long, hissing exhalation of breath from between Lippe's closed teeth and saw his huge face loom up through a haze of tobacco smoke until the eyes were only inches away from him.

'Mystery piled on mystery, Schmidt!' the old man whispered hoarsely. His face expressed surprise but not astonishment.

The observation deck became level again. Dilke let go of the foot-bar and got to his knees then to his feet and collapsed into the seat, dazed and exhausted by his falls.

Lippe's face receded and Dilke heard the sound of a drawer being opened.

Then a great eye filled Dilke's whole field of vision; a

black centre, ringed with brown, and surrounded by yellowish white. The powerful magnifying lens revealed it in brilliant detail. The dark brown iris was flecked with amber. Blood vessels were coiled like snakes beneath the translucent ivory surface of the eyeball. The fluid which lubricated the eye had carried scum along the lower lid and deposited it as a soft plug in the corner. The great hand which held the Aid shook. Dilke hung on to the sides of the chair and heard a gentle wheezing laugh.

'Look, Schmidt!'

The professor handed the reading-glass to his assistant and the second eye which stared at Dilke was bright and cold and wide with curiosity.

The atmosphere in the room was tense with excitement. The two men stared through the perspex at Dilke like zoologists who have just discovered a new species of bug. 'So perfect, Schmidt! So *small!*' breathed the old man.

Miniaturization was not news to them; rumours about it had reached them through the international scientific grapevine, and they gazed at the speck of human life on the desk with ardent curiosity.

Lippe leaned forward intently and speculated enthusiastically and lengthily about the phenomenon of a man reduced to the size of an insect.

Was the process one of reduction: the making small of a grown man? he mused. Or was it a repressive process: curtailing the growth of a test-tube human, perhaps one grown in the laboratory from a single body cell?

Was chemistry involved? Surgery? Radiation? Molecular transmutation?

'Perhaps our little man can tell us, Schmidt, and we

might dabble in the field ourselves! Or we can employ him to find out!' Professor Lippe smiled down at the still, small figure below him. 'Espionage is not an employment for the scrupulous. Can your services be bought, my little investigator?' The voice was mocking. 'Will you work for a new master?'

Rage swept away Dilke's paralysing exhaustion.

He slammed down the volume control lever and snarled: 'You dirty, sodding, murderous bastard!'

The invective was commonplace, but the bitter venom with which he spat it out made it electrifying.

Heinrich Lippe's smile vanished. His face became a cold expressionless mask. He lowered his pipe slowly and deliberately on to the desk. There was a click when it touched the desk top, then there was silence except for the soft whistle of breath through his nostrils.

'Leave me, Schmidt.'

The German unfroze, then faded into the dark and the room door opened and closed with hardly a sound.

Heinrich Lippe's eyes glittered in their shadowed sockets, his mouth was a thin compressed line. Dilke heard a distant wheezing and sighing, deep in the man's great lungs and was conscious of a curious smell: a thin, sour, insidious smell; the stale, oppressive odour of old age and decay. Dilke stared hypnotically into the black pupils – windows into the dark interiors of the great visual organs – and felt cold fear.

PART THREE

7

Lippe carried the Aid from his room, along a corridor and into the dark conference chamber.

There was a click and a rectangle of light glowed beneath the surface of the long table. Recessed into its middle section was a box with hinged glass covers, like a museum showcase or a display unit for jewellery. Lippe raised a cover, unclipped the hearing-aid dome and, with a tap of his forefinger, precipitated Dilke on to the floor of the box.

Dilke rolled over and over then scrambled to his feet. The lid closed with a thud; Dilke heard a hiss and felt pressure on his eardrums as a vacuum-seal made the box airtight. It was like a great glass-roofed stadium almost a foot high and a yard wide. He could not see its length as the single strip-light on the end wall left it in shadow. A laboratory beaker half-full of liquid and another containing crystals stood side-by-side; above them a rubber glove protruded stiffly from the wall. Dilke went quickly towards the concealment of the shadows, hoping to find a way of escape. But a wall of glass blocked off the end of the box, stretching the full width and meeting the roof high above. Dilke peered through the transparent barrier; a crawling pattern of black shapes moved in the shadows; he pressed against the glass and blinkered his eyes against the reflected light with cupped hands. The shapes moved swiftly and aimlessly over floor and walls and roof; Dilke's hair rose on his neck and scalp.

Two huge multicellular eyes suddenly appeared and stared at him. Dilke recoiled with a startled cry. The armoured form of an insect reared up and glared down at him; he heard the rattle of its claws and, muffled by the barrier between them, its high-pitched electronic screech. The shapes beyond the creature froze into stillness, they stood erect with antennae spread like horns above their plated heads.

South American army ants! Carnivorous predators. Nomadic destroyers of all living things in their path. As Dilke retreated they came to the wall in a rush and covered it with their clinging black bodies. A multitude of glowing eyes followed him as he ran to conceal himself behind a beaker.

Then the red glove projecting from the wall above him quivered and turned a shade darker as a hand was thrust into it from outside. The glove picked up a beaker and meticulously poured a gin-clear liquid on to the beaker of crystals. There was a chemical explosion within the vessel, shattered crystals spun and dissolved in the swirling liquid, and from its spitting surface green fumes ascended to the roof then thinned to a yellow mist as they spread in the air.

Dilke gasped breathlessly like a man submerged in icy water. Ice filled his body and brain. His heart hammered at his ribs. The world lurched sideways one step. The floor moved in waves, in rhythm with the rapid pulse of his blood.

An irregular patch appeared on his field of vision, an

opening on to infinity which grew in size and obscured the mass of ants which clung to the glass wall. He discerned the faint outline of a human ear within the expanding jigsaw shape. More and more of a face in profile was revealed: it was Heinrich Lippe, his head tilted down, a book held near to his eyes. A boiling rage drove the icy numbness from Dilke's senses. He lifted his eyes from the hallucinatory image and saw the real features of the professor looking down through the glass roof. The great head was very close to the glass, breath from the simian lips condensed on its surface.

Dilke glared furiously into the peering eyes, then, hearing a growing roar of sound, he stared towards the distant insects. The wall which held them back was coming down like a great glass drawbridge! Ants on its upper edge were already tumbling to the floor and racing towards him; as the wall fell with a crash the rest swarmed after them.

Then an extraordinary thing happened.

Before they reached Dilke the forerunners abruptly stopped, turned and attacked each other ferociously. Within seconds, fighting spread to the thousands which followed. Though he was familiar with ant warfare Dilke had never seen them wage civil war. This conflict was infinitely more savage than any he had seen before. Through a curtain of yellow vapour he saw the raging black mass coalesce into a thick rope of screaming insects which writhed and heaved up almost to the roof. Dilke watched the erupting violence and shared the furious rage of the insects. The needle-sharp screeching and the crackle of breaking armour slowly diminished, then the orgy of mutual slaughter finished with the same abruptness with which it began.

A whisper grew until it filled the chamber with the

sound of an electric fan; the mist thinned and was drawn away to a grille in the wall. Suddenly drained of feeling, Dilke sat down.

The air was clear and there was silence. Dilke lay on his back and stared up at the roof. His eyes were sore, his lips and mouth parched, his unclenched jaws ached from the tension of his dissipated rage, now replaced by a feeling of weary inertia.

The lid of the box was raised, the grey smudge of Lippe's face floated in the darkness above and his great hand came down, delicately holding a matchstick as big as a tree trunk between finger and thumb. He lowered the match to within half-an-inch of Dilke and tapped it on the floor.

'Mount up, Insektenmann!'

Dilke went to it obediently, stretched out on it and clutched its rough surface. It was lifted slowly into the air; Dilke saw below him, banked up across the floor of the box, a glistening pile of wreckage lying in a flood of insect blood and excreta. Then the matchstick sailed out of the box and was gently deposited in a tray which lay on the table.

Heinrich Lippe returned to his office to put away the tray in a drawer, and during the short time before Lippe went to his bed Dilke looked for a way up the high walls of the tray. Then the desk lamp went out and the light which shone through the slit at the top of the closed drawer was extinguished, leaving Dilke in total darkness.

He sat on the matchstick and waited for his eyes to adjust to the dark but it remained impenetrably black. He shuffled forward cautiously until he came to a wall and ran his hands over its cold surface, searching for irregularities; it was smooth and unclimbable. He explored the perimeter of the tray for an hour, then squatted in an angle between two walls until the cold struck through his clothes; he regretted leaving the bulk and comparative warmth of the matchstick and walked blindly into the dark to find it.

But he found no match and did not come again to a wall. Though he knew that the walls existed and that he was moving in circles it seemed that he was lost on a limitless plain. To find the great block of timber became an obsession. It was something desirable, tangible, an island in an endless sea of black ice, a sanctuary.

He walked till he was weary, then sat down.

He rose and walked again, then stretched out on the icy surface until the cold drove him to his knees.

It may be only a hand-stretch away! Tormented by the belief that he was within easy reach of the match he crawled forward and swung his arms wildly to left and right.

He lay down at last with his legs drawn up, his forehead touching his knees, his arms around his head, his fists clenched.

It was a long night of shivering semi-consciousness and of bad dreams filled with black ants.

Dilke was curled up like an embryo. He opened an eye and lay still with his right cheek against the steel floor. The matchstick was a hundred paces away. He uncurled his body and the air chilled his thighs, belly and chest; even his thumbs, now exposed by his open fingers, felt the coldness of the air.

The great pine matchstick gleamed dimly in the grey light which filtered into the drawer. Groaning at the cramp in his legs he went to it and lay in a stupor on its rough surface.

83

Bellamy's death, the yellow gas, the warring ants and his hallucination, the nightmares from which he had just awakened merged into a series of events in which the real and the unreal were indistinguishable. He lay and thought of the dangers which faced him. He was the captive of a man with a disturbing division of character: behind benevolence and an eye for beauty lay ruthlessness and an appetite for persecution. Dilke sat up and squatted on the log and regretted his rejection of Lippe's invitation to act the double agent. It was an indiscretion he would not repeat if the offer was made again: agreement would give him an opportunity to escape, but was the old man ingenuous enough to let him go?

It was eight o'clock; Dilke renewed his search for a way out of the tray but found no more than his blind reconnaissance in the night had shown him: the walls could not be climbed. He was imprisoned in a yard as big as a football pitch, with smooth, steel walls ten times his height.

At nine he heard footsteps, the drawer slid open and Lippe reached in and picked up the tray. The professor wore a white towelling robe and his hair was still wet from the shower; his expression was calm, almost benign. He looked into the tray for a long moment then took it through the glass door and carried it across the sunlit terrace. Dilke felt the shock of impact as the tray was put down on the low terrace wall.

Lippe raised his voice above its normal hoarse whisper to greet someone Dilke could not see; Dilke heard the slap of bare feet approaching and the head and shoulder of the murderer appeared above the wall of the tray. The man ducked his head obsequiously and stood at a little distance; Lippe seated himself beside the tray, took a reading-glass from his pocket and peered down through it.

'Good morning, Insektenmann!'

The half-breed watched the old man with wonder on his fat face.

The professor delivered a wheezing monologue to the tray in a voice which was touched with regret.

He spoke of the sad decline in business morals; he asked how business could survive in the absence of integrity and honest dealing; he categorized industrial spies as the anarchists of the business world.

Lippe's manner became colder. 'Your master pretended that he wished to purchase patent rights when his intention was to steal them; rights which were the result of many years of my work and invention. If a thief takes from me that which is mine, where lies my just reward?'

The half-breed crept forward and stared over the edge of the tray.

'Your master was a parasite on the body of industry!'
Lippe was not displeased with the analogy; a smile moved his lips, then abruptly disappeared.

'And your master has had retribution. "Denn all Schuld rächt sich auf Erden." For all guilt is punished on earth, as Goethe puts it!'

Lippe shifted slightly to move his shadow from the tray and silently studied Dilke through the magnifying lens. Dilke shaded his eyes against the dazzling sun and stared up into the great face; sweat covered his body and fear twisted in the pit of his stomach.

'Denn all Schuld rächt sich auf Erden!' Lippe dwelt fondly on each syllable. 'Those who share guilt must also share punishment. In all justice, the lesser parasite must share retribution with the greater one. Are not the English the apostles of fair play?'

The huge lens moved and Dilke no longer saw the magnified eye. A blast of heat passed over him as the spot of concentrated sunlight flew across the floor of the tray and stopped fifty paces away.

'Even an English *insect* must have fair play!'

Insect was given a mocking emphasis. Malevolence glittered in the monkey-brown eyes; the reading-glass in the great hand moved slowly through the air and beneath it a pool of concentrated heat and light moved over the floor of the tray. Dilke crouched beside the matchstick and stared at the approaching incandescence. Blinding light flooded the crimson match-head as the bar of sunlight struck it.

With a roar like an ignited furnace the great ball of phosphorus erupted into flame.

Dilke turned and ran.

Spurts of white fire changed to a blaze of yellow edged with blue, which advanced along the great log, driving steaming moisture from its interior.

Dilke stood at a distance and felt the transmitted heat in the steel underfoot. The plating buckled and split with a sharp report under the combined heat of blazing sunspot and radiant chemical fire. The tray was plastic masquerading as steel, covered with a microscopically thin skin of metal. Molten plastic boiled up like tar between the curled-back metal edges, thick as ship's plating to Dilke. A bubble formed, grew rapidly, then collapsed with a dull explosion.

Dilke watched the timber fade from red to silvery black. Astonished by the violence of the conflagration and at the transformation it had caused he went towards the burnt-out log; its straight, squared-off bulk was now a twisted hulk of charcoal, the charred wood creaked and ticked like an old clock as it cooled. The neck behind the bulbous match-head suddenly fractured and the stick separated and rolled over with a crash. Fire still glowed at the centre of the match-head, visible through deep holes which pitted its surface. Spent gas streamed from the holes as the glow faded, and when it finally died a plume of smoke flew up. Dilke watched its swift ascent into the blue sky with dazed wonder. The smell of burnt phosphorus hung in the air and stung the lining of his nostrils.

The fire was out.

A blast of heat struck his back and he jerked his head round. The pool of burning light waited behind him. He stepped back hastily and slitted his eyes against its shimmering brilliance. As he walked away it followed him at a little distance; he changed direction but still it kept pace. It gave a disturbing illusion of conscious purpose, there was something dog-like in its movements. He quickened his walk and the spot went smoothly with him down the length of the tray, but its speed slowly increased until instead of following, it forced him to walk faster.

Suddenly it disappeared from behind and reappeared in a flash before him. Dilke fell back, it moved round him in a semicircle then forced him towards a corner of the tray where it left him, to float away over the steel surface in a series of lazy arabesques.

He tensely watched its dazzling movements then raised his eyes to the lens in Lippe's great hand. Amusement marked the shadowed face beyond the moving glass; the old man's eyes were hooded and a smile of anticipation curled his lips.

The sunspot increased its speed until Dilke could

hardly follow its flashing curves and loops, then it zig-zagged towards him, climbed the wall at his back and drove him out of the corner.

The elegant calligraphy was finished.

Now the spot drove him across the tray in short, straight lines, turning him brutally at every dozen steps. He ran until the breath rasped in his throat and his body ached with strain.

The eastern wall of the tray threw a shadow which he ran desperately towards. Dilke thought his heart would burst; despite the scorching heat his heavy legs moved more slowly, and the spot slowed down to keep pace. He ran out of the sun and collapsed in the shadow of the wall; the sunspot was cut off and the steel on which he lay cooled his burning flesh. He lay back in an agony of breathlessness and glared at the sky. The hand and glass had vanished, now the giant head of his tormentor appeared over the top of the wall.

The smile had gone from Lippe's face, replaced by a stare of rapt attention. His eyes were wide and fixed, dark pupils centred within circles of white; blood suffused his sallow cheeks and his mouth was set in a tight line.

The half-breed had come nearer to watch this sport of insect-baiting; he looked into the miniature arena and his monstrous body shook with suppressed giggles.

A thumb hooked over the edge of the tray and turned it round, sunshine replaced shadow, the sunspot reappeared and drove Dilke to the middle of the tray. He went on trembling legs, tripping, almost falling, making short runs forward to recover his balance, staggering to right and left. The sun had grown in strength as it ascended, and the tray had absorbed its direct heat and that which had been focused on it by the lens. The ho air with which Dilke laboured to fill his lungs dried his throat; the light which was reflected between floor and walls blinded him. At the centre of the arena the spot left him. He wiped sweat from his eyes and watched it travel to the nearest wall then turn and begin a clockwise circuit of the tray. He followed its progress, turning on his heel until he almost fell with dizziness, then he stood and watched it flash past for lap after lap.

Each time it passed it was a little nearer. He watched it with dull anticipation. The torment he had suffered had progressed with a sort of formality. He was at the centre of the decreasing circles and he recognized that the game was near its end.

8

The headquarters of Compañía Peruana de Plásticos lay in a region with a summer rainfall of almost nil, but a freak cloud had crossed the Andes during the night and now floated five miles above the foothills.

This patch of cirrus saved Mathew Dilke. As it drifted across the face of the sun the temperature in the tray fell and the spot of blistering light which raced closer and closer to him was reduced to a soft-edged glow. His crouching tormentor straightened with a grunt and stared up at the veiled sun; a breath of air lifted the old man's fine, white hair and settled it slowly across his forehead; he threw it back with a gesture of impatience and swore in German. The same moving air cooled Dilke's sweating face and body; a spark of will-to-live sent him staggering towards the burnt-out matchstick; hoping, despairingly, that its blackened remains would give him concealment or protection. But as he stumbled along its shrivelled length he knew that it could neither hide nor shield him from his executioner.

The cloud would pass; the sun would blaze; the spot would return.

Then he saw the hole!

It was a crater four millimetres across, narrowing to a hole little more than a millimetre wide – remnant of the molten plastic bubble which had swelled and burst in the heat of the erupting match-head. Dilke stepped down into the crater without hesitation. His legs, hips and torso went through the hole but he stuck at the shoulders. The plastic had not fully set; a band of intense heat enclosed his chest and he squirmed in panic and stretched his arms upwards. The plastic yielded, and he slid through the hole and dropped to the ground, landing heavily on his back. He had fallen from light into dark and for a moment hardly knew where he was. The vast floor of the tray was above him, supported on longitudinal ribs. He sat up and shook his head.

He had escaped, but now trembled with indecision; he longed to remain in dark concealment, but knew that to stay would lead to his recapture. He was in a world of giants, of men like mountains; the massive structure under which he hid would soon be lifted to reveal the insect beneath. He scrambled up in fear and ran under the low ceiling towards the light.

He ran from under the tray as the sun came out and a furious exclamation showed that his disappearance had been discovered. The great tray became airborne in the professor's grasp, and Dilke was bowled over by the gale which was sucked up beneath it; Lippe raised it against the sky, saw the pinhole of light and flung it aside. His angry face bent low.

The top of the wall was smooth, without cover or cracks into which Dilke could crawl; he ran towards the edge of the parapet and saw the lake far below at the base of the sloping wall. A shadow fell; the dark shape

of a hand came down like a fall of rock. Dilke saw nico-
tined channels on a great descending thumb; he
screamed, ran, and tumbled over the edge of the parapet.

After a free fall of several inches Dilke hit the outcurv-
ing slope and tumbled and rolled interminably until he
plunged into the lake.

The fall battered him almost senseless. He lay in the
shallows, soaking his scorched body, until the sound of
Lippe's cross voice slowly entered his consciousness. He
gulped water thirstily, sat up, and stared at the sweeping
white slope down which he had fallen.

Urged on by Lippe, the half-breed was descending the
wall.

Dilke ran from the water. The shore was pure white,
starkly revealing his dark figure. A raft of dead leaves
lay on the lake; he leapt back into the water, swam towards it and pulled himself on to the decaying mass. He
scrambled from one sodden leaf to the next, sliding and
slipping into slime-filled pores, until he reached the
middle of the raft where he was almost invisible against
its dark surface.

The half-breed backed clumsily down the short slope,
keeping a fingertip balance on its curved surface, and
stood ankle-deep in the water. Nodding and grinning at
Lippe's scolding instructions he bent and searched the
shore; then, obedient to the old man's directions, he
waded towards the floating leaves, cautiously sliding his
feet along the sloping bottom until he was almost knee
deep.

A surge of water rolled under the raft and threw Dilke
down; he lay in frozen stillness as the half-breed loomed
overhead. The raft covered an irregular square yard of
water and the man laughed and slapped at it with

gigantic fat hand; he had enjoyed Lippe's sport with the insect! he enjoyed joining the game!

A shout from the old man quietened him. He crouched to examine the debris, then took a floating twig and raked with it, carefully detaching individual leaves and examining them minutely.

Far out on the lake a ruffled patch moved across its surface as if brushed by the wind. The patch grew bigger, moved fitfully to north and south, formed an arrowhead of broken water and flashed towards the western shore.

The shoal hit the man's legs when his face was only inches away from Dilke.

Shock and bewilderment contorted the huge features. Bursting internal pressure swelled head and neck. The mouth gaped open, ropes of spittle hung down from its roof to the tongue glistening behind a wall of broken teeth. Bellamy's murderer had breakfasted on black beans, remnants filled the craters in his back molars; the smell of bean pulp and dental decay fouled the air. Sweat flooded his greasy skin and his swarthy face turned purple. He straightened up, then toppled backwards. Beneath the surface of the lake the fish had stripped his legs almost to the bone; blood from severed arteries darkened the water which boiled around his knees.

It was the fall of an empire of flesh. Only one message flashed along the network of nerves, one sensation raged in the chambers of the brain. Pain – savage, ripping, tearing, wholly unbearable pain – blocked all other feelings and paralysed all action. Rivers of blood drained from the vast arterial labyrinth. A shuddering inhalation whistled into the cavernous lungs. The throat locked on a rising scream.

Dilke watched him disappear into the water. The

delayed scream came up as a muffled explosion like the upsurge of a depth-charge, then a vast arm rose from the depths. A steel wristwatch on a braided steel band flashed in the sun, the jagged white teeth of a fish were sunk into the meat of the forearm. Arm, watch, fish, flailed through the air in a ponderous arc.

Before it hit the surface of the lake in a cloud of spray Dilke recognized the fish's massively overdeveloped lower jaw, the razor-edged triangular teeth, and the furious eyes beneath bone-plated brows. He saw a flashing swarm of fish in the turbulent water. Heinrich Lippe's pets were piranhas; living meat had transformed the lethargic carp-like creatures of yesterday into killers.

The old man leaned far out over the parapet and stared down with the same rapt attention he had shown when poised to exterminate Dilke.

Waves tossed Dilke's raft of leaves towards the lakeside; he crossed the waterlogged mass, stumbled through shallows and ran along the edge of the water away from the professor's looming figure. Successive wind-blown tides had thrown up lines of scum on to the lakeside. He kept close to one of these tidemarks to lessen the risk of detection and ran until his new-found energy faded.

He looked back, saw that Lippe still watched the swirling water with fixed concentration, then hurried on till he had travelled several yards along the shore.

When Dilke stopped to rest, the spectator on the parapet had relaxed and was seated on the wall lighting his pipe. When it was lit he tossed the match away; it hissed into the water and floated over the place where the halfbreed had gone down. The smoker turned from the lake and moved slowly from Dilke's view, leaving a trail of tobacco smoke behind.

The sun blazed on the white beach and glittered on

the water. Dilke sat in a state of shock in the shelter of a dead leaf, dazed by the disasters he had experienced. Though his unaided movement was now extraordinarily slow after the speed he had known as Bellamy's passenger, the death of his companion had not properly sunk in. Dilke had not yet readjusted to the micro-world; the leaf beneath which he sat was part of a long line of washed-up leaves and stalks and small twigs which had caked together in a series of caverns resembling a street of half-demolished slum dwellings.

The afternoon advanced. He had not eaten for a day and he felt the dull ache of hunger. He searched the shore listlessly, and unsuccessfully, for food and returned to his hovel, then lay back wearily and looked up at a patch of sky through a hole in the leaf. Its cellular fabric had rotted away revealing structural ribs like rafters in the roof of a derelict house. A cloud of gnats danced in the blue; vague regret that he had no repellent was followed by remembrance that the insects were not the tiny irritants of his life before miniaturization. To one of his stature they were winged cattle.

Dilke slept badly, and went out early into the dawn light. Mist shrouded the lake. He was stiff and sore and his cat-suit was torn and dirty. He stripped, washed the garment in the shallows and threw it on the shore, then waded out and washed himself. Beneath the dirt lay evidence of his fall down the wall; spreading bruises darkened his battered and shaken body, and he discovered an injury which shock had concealed from him. He had burned his right arm on hot plastic while escaping through the hole in the tray. The skin was seared from wrist to shoulder; he squatted and carefully bathed the arm.

Then he felt the water stir around him with a barely perceptible movement, and was seized by a premonition of danger. He looked up slowly.

The head of a freshwater lizard had risen from the lake. Brilliant green, scaled, studded with warts, crested like a creature from pre-history, the monster's eyes were fixed on him. He was petrified by its closeness and its size. Micro-man and reptile were motionless for a long minute, then Dilke edged backwards to the shore. The leathery throat jerked; the bony jaws, armed with teeth like knives, opened; a hissing roar came from the gaping mouth and blew spray into Dilke's face. He turned and ran. A surge of water pursued him as he raced out of the shallows and up the shore. The slap of webbed feet grew louder as he fled. He glanced back, the lumbering monster was seventy millimetres long. He darted into a hole in a mound of rubbish, but it forced its blunt head after him and scrabbled with clawed feet. He was in a sloping shaft which opened on to the surface of the mound. He climbed up, leapt out, and made off across its rough surface; the head of the lizard erupted from the hole behind him.

A deserted snail shell lay half-buried in the mound, its cup filled to the brim with water. Dilke climbed on to the lip, dived, swam two strokes underwater and surfaced inside the shell. A shadow fell across the shell and a violent blow rocked it. Dilke looked up and saw the shape of the lizard's foot on the translucent surface. Terrified that the brute would reach in and claw him out, he scrambled from the big antechamber into the inner spiral. Here water had not penetrated; he crawled round the narrowing passage until he could go no further, then squeezed into the blind end and listened to the rasp of belly scales on the shell's exterior.

The slap of water in the entrance chamber died away, Dilke's breathing became more regular, the light which penetrated the walls of his refuge grew brighter. Dilke listened for sounds from outside but all was silent. He touched the smooth mother-of-pearl surface of the shell with his fingertips and watched the second hand of his watch.

An hour passed. The sun was up and the air he breathed became hotter and hotter. He could bear the confinement no longer, he slid out of the coiled labyrinth and re-entered the domed vestibule; most of the water had spilled from the shell, Dilke waded cautiously through what remained and peered out fearfully. Beyond the piled debris on which the shell lay, the beach sloped down to the lake. Nothing moved but points of sunlight on the water. Dilke jumped out of the shell and ran across the hills of rubbish and up the sloping wall.

Dilke looked down on the deceptively innocent lake and sweated over the memory of his escape from the water lizard. The lake to him was an inland sea twenty micromiles across – a perfect circle within the crater's rim – and the frontage of Lippe's terrace covered a dozen micro-miles of its circumference.

Behind him the cliff-like wall swept up to an unclimbable overhang.

He looked to right and left at the long arc of the terrace and saw that a metal framework jutted out from its southern extremity and projected over the water. He shaded his eyes and stared at the distant pier for a long moment, then set off towards it. This could be his way of escape from a barren coast which promised only violent death or slow starvation.

*　　　*　　　*

Dilke was glad to lie in the shadow of the steel platform after a two-hour walk in the hot sun. From a half-dozen micro-miles away he had not realized how massive the structure was. From beneath, it seemed a mile high. Though it did not lead directly to the terrace it *was* attached to the terrace's southern wall. If he climbed it he could reach the top of the wall; from there he could descend to the terrace itself.

He looked with curiosity at the structure. What was it for? A ramp of old railway sleepers led to an enclosed platform from which a sort of chute entered the water at a steep angle. The chute was too steep for launching a boat and was too narrow anyway. It was surfaced with metal rollers of the sort on which heavy cases were moved, or like the chutes used for dipping cattle.

No matter! The thing was to climb it.

The end which overhung the lake rested on steel legs which stood in water; the legs which supported the other end were almost hidden in thick vegetation. To start his climb he must either take a swim or make a jungle trip.

He decided to swim. The girders rose from the water about a quarter of a micro-mile away; he told himself that he could do it in twenty minutes.

A criss-cross of vast struts joined the two steel legs; they were pitted with rust and would be easy to climb; he would take a zig-zag route up the angles they made. He looked again at the water, which was as smooth and as clear as glass. An empty beer-can floated a few hundred millimetres from the shore; a wasp landed on it, neatly folded its wings and bustled inside through a hole in the top of the great cylinder.

Seeds like miniature coconuts lay in the shallows; one of them had rooted in sludge at the water's edge and had grown a leaf as big as his hand. He pulled it up, greedily ate the main root then threw the rest away and stepped forward.

The wasp came out of the hole, wandered aimlessly around the top of the beer-can and fell into the water. A minnow shot out of the shadow beneath the can and seized the wasp by a wing; a dozen more fish which had been lurking in the shadow of the girders flashed towards the wasp like sharks attacking a bullock. Within seconds its frantic buzzing was silenced; Dilke saw its sinking yellow-and-black body – stripped of wings, legs and antennae – at the centre of a fighting mass of fish. He fled from the water, paced up and down swearing nervously, then made off up the slope towards the tropical forest which concealed the other pair of supporting girders.

Beneath the sunlit leaves was a dark jungle of rampant plants and rotting vegetation.

'Back to bloody first base!' he swore, recalling his first days of miniaturization when, equally naked, equally defenceless, he had entered the riotous and roaring world of plant and insect life. But that had been an English country garden; the humid darkness into which he now reluctantly crept was infinitely more menacing.

The hum of insect activity grew louder as he went more deeply into the interior. He climbed the pale stem and lay concealed within the curled leaf of a pigmy fern; he saw the glint of huge cylindrical shapes piled mountain-high beneath the dark canopy of leaves. The smell of stale beer and the rank ammonia smell of stale urine filled the air. Most of the cans were rust-red; but on some of them gigantic, enamelled words were discernible: *Cerveza Primera* and *Cerveza Superbia*, and a gilt-edged *High Life: the champagne of beers* from Milwaukee, U.S.A.

Swarming on and around and inside the mountain was a mass of insects. Hover-flies delicately sucked beer and saliva from the rims of cans. Beetles rushed in and out of the cans carrying crystals of sugar. Ants fed indiscriminately on loot and looters alike. Spiders descended on the alcoholics which crawled aimlessly on the forest floor, and carried them off clicking and chittering weakly.

Dilke silently withdrew, leaving behind the amplified drinking songs of wasps and wild bees booming from the interiors of the vast containers.

Dilke stood in dismay between the jungle and the sea and looked up at the unattainable bridge of steel high above. He turned again to the green wall; tropical briars had pushed up suckers from the earth at the edge of the jungle. The shoots climbed vertically then curved away and entwined with more mature plants.

Dilke saw that the tangle of briars and creepers, of stems and leaves and branches, grew as high as the terrace wall. The lower depths of this tropical forest in miniature were too dark and dangerous for him. His eyes followed the sweeping briars ascending through sunlit leaves: *this* was the route he must take. It would be bloody rough going but it was the only way. He returned to the shore, found another germinating seed and filled his belly with its roots and pulpy interior. Still he put it off. He washed his sweating body, took a long drink, then he made for the nearest briar at the edge of the jungle.

The inch-thick trunk of the briar was studded with huge polished thorns and covered with lesser spikes. Dilke climbed too fast and after an hour was exhausted. But his growing doubts about the route vanished when, from a resting place astride a thorn, he looked down on the lake and saw dark shapes lurking in the shadow of the floating beer can, and heard the distant drone of insects from the interior of the jungle. He had started late and at sunset he had not found a refuge for the night. He scrambled upwards, came to a leaf stem just before the brief tropical twilight gave way to total darkness, and settled down thankfully in the depression where stem joined trunk.

He slept fitfully. Disturbed by the throbbing of his injured arm, which had been inflamed by the rigours of climbing, he stared into the night.

He could not dress the wound. If it turned septic he would be unable to climb, unable to find food. He shivered in the dark. The arm could kill him.

The sky turned slowly from black to grey. Dilke watched the dawn of a new Peruvian day without enthusiasm.

At the end of the stem on which he crouched the great leaf stirred in the morning breeze. There was a movement on its dark underside and something travelled along the middle of the leaf, stepping with circumspection around the hooked thorns which grew from the main rib, and crawled up over the leaf's edge. The diminutive bug tentatively pierced the green surface with its hollow beak then trundled down the sloping stem towards Dilke.

It was an infant sapsucker in a pretty shade of green, with liquid black eyes like a seal pup. Dilke plucked it off the stem, beat its head against the trunk and had his first breakfast for three days; the tender meat within its as yet unhardened casing was as sweet as the sap on which it had been raised.

Dilke examined his arm; touched the swollen flesh around the burn and looked for signs of corruption; the wound was weeping freely but its colour was not bad.

Work it off! he thought grimly and started up the vertical trunk.

Steak for breakfast improved his stamina. He reached the point, late in the afternoon, where the briar arched towards the thicket and climbing grew easier as the briar became progressively less vertical. He spent a second night in the fork of a leaf stem but no windfall came his way in the morning. He continued his journey faint with hunger **and** tormented by thirst, his mood made no sweeter by knowing that beneath his feet sugar-water flowed in abundance.

At last he entered the fringe of the thicket and the shadows which dappled the path gave some shelter from the sun. He came suddenly upon an adult sapsucker in a patch of shadow. The bug was motionless, with its big head lowered menacingly. He leapt back in panic then saw the thick beak sunk into the briar and heard the heavy pulse of rising fluid. He approached cautiously and gave the beast an experimental kick on the side of the head; the sound of pumping stopped. He kicked hard and repeatedly at the beak; the bug slowly raised its head, the beak withdrew with a sucking sound and clear sap welled up and ran round the curve of the briar's trunk. Dilke retreated behind a thorn, the creature lumbered away, and he threw himself down and eagerly drank the cool, sweet liquid. Soon the overflow stopped and the hole dried up, but he had drunk enough. He stood up and looked hungrily at the oxlike bug which was sinking another well not far away, then turned and reluctantly continued his journey. The beast was too big and powerful for him to kill without a weapon.

The leaves grew thicker, excluding the light, and touching the briar in places. Unnerved by the rustling movement and calls of unseen creatures he hurried on to come at last to light and space. There were vast shad-owed depths below and open sky far above. It was a break in the dense vegetation, a sort of leafy canyon, bridged across by many briars like his own. A butterfly was sunning on one of them. A cluster of orchids grew up from the shadows; the nearest one almost touched the briar. He walked out and looked down at the huge yellow bloom and inhaled its exotic perfume.

9

High in the thicket a female wolf-spider sprawled upon a leaf. She lay quite still with her heavy belly pressed to its surface and her eight clawed legs clutching its edges. A baking heat beat down on the leaf and penetrated the silk cocoon which was bound tight to its underside. All morning the spider had felt vague movements beneath her; now, with the sun at its hottest, the twitching and shaking were unmistakable.

She lowered her head, sank her great fangs into the leaf and ripped a hole in its surface. A horde of young spiders erupted from the hole, swarmed across their fearsome mother, then scrambled up the branch and gathered on the edge of its topmost leaf. There, jostling for position, they lifted their backsides and extruded silk from their spinnerets. These shining, lighter-than-air filaments floated away and as each spider judged that the moment was right it stopped spinning, grabbed the cord and was pulled off the leaf into the air.

They drifted south in hundreds in a slow descent towards the surface of the lake. Dilke saw them pass overhead; sunlit spots too high to distinguish as living creatures.

The last of the brood to leave the launching pad lost their buoyancy in a pocket of cooler air and dropped into Dilke's valley. Dozens of them came down like paratroopers; a few vanished into the void below, others hung by their silk cords from arching briars; one crashed on to Dilke's footbridge.

He saw a squat brown body on eight straddled legs and four pairs of black eyes glaring amongst bristling ginger hair. Casting off its rope it whirled towards him along the briar. Dilke saw needle-like fangs; he half-jumped, half-fell on to the lip of the orchid and the thing shot past and disappeared amongst the leaves.

Some spiders continued their descent in fast, controlled falls at the end of freshly-spun cords. Others climbed their ropes like acrobats and raced into hiding along the briar stems. A butterfly which was sunning on a briar, startled by whistling and grunting invaders which scuttled between her legs and under her massive abdomen, took to the air with a clatter of wings.

There were spiders everywhere. Dilke looked around wildly then ran up the lip of the orchid, dived into its throat and tumbled into the heart of the flower.

He lay in a translucent chamber with velvety walls. A soft and shadowless light revealed curved, primrose-yellow surfaces flecked with gold. Pollen grains as big as grapefruit and as yellow as butter hung in clusters overhead; he took one and lay back and ate its sweet flesh.

All was dreamlike, luminous, silent – a million miles from the harsh world outside. He fell asleep and lay without movement through the afternoon and evening. When moonlight filtered through the chamber walls he drifted up through layers of sleep, diver-like, in slow stages, to float at the edge of consciousness. Strange sounds filled the air: slithering notes descended haltingly to soft groans, then ascended to long-drawn muted squeals.

He gazed through heavy-lidded eyes at the golden fruit, now silvered, which clustered under the pale dome then closed his half-closed eyes and sank again into black unconsciousness.

He awoke at dawn, sprawled on the soft floor of the flower's interior, freed by his long sleep from the state of tension and fearfulness which had possessed him since Bellamy's death.

He yawned and stretched luxuriously then crawled out of the flower and stood on its broad lip. Mist filled the air; huge pearls of dew hung from the arched briars; a pale moth silently flew down to its dark hiding-place in the depths of the leafy canyon.

He looked around. Something very strange had happened. The bridge, from which he had tumbled to evade the young wolf-spider, had vanished.

He went to the edge of the petal and peered down. The briar was now more than three inches beneath him – a hundred micro-feet below the level of the flower.

The orchid had grown. The mysterious sounds he had heard in the twilight of his sleep had been the sounds of its growth: a glutinous music of oozing sap, of cellular movement and sliding vegetable tissue.

He was marooned on an aerial platform, but he felt no impulse to escape. To Dilke, the flower's inner chamber was a refuge, not a prison.

High above, the first rays of sunlight slanted into the valley; he smiled dreamily into mist made golden by the morning light. He drank from a pool of dew in the curled edge of the petal then concealed himself in the flower's narrow throat and watched the awakening of a new day.

A hunting wasp cruised along the green canyon. A lacewing darted out of the leaves, crossed the valley, and disappeared into the opposite wall of foliage. The courtship of two butterflies perched on a branch was interrupted by rival males; the female flirted her wings and flew off in a storm of competing lovers.

More butterflies appeared. In England Dilke had never seen such extraordinary diversity of size, shape and colour. Swallowtails as big as clipper ships, fritillaries as neat and fast as racing skiffs. By midday the valley was alive with them and the orchid swayed in the turbulence of their flight. The mottled and striped and spotted wings blurred into a whirl of gorgeous colours; perfume from the scented wing-scales which showered from the great creatures filled the air.

The orchid had faced the east at dawn but as it turned westwards in pursuit of the sun Dilke was given a slowly-changing view of the precipitous green wall before him. Foliage which had appeared dense and impenetrable was now revealed to his leisurely gaze as a broken screen through which he could see a three-dimensional labyrinth of leafy avenues and clearings hung with tropical flowers. Butterflies perched on the flowers sipping nectar. Others, fresh from the ardours of mating, sprayed newly fertilized eggs into the air. Some (with a less random maternity) gravely extruded their eggs on to leaves and stems with mathematical precision.

Dilke watched it all with fascination until the light began to fail and the butterflies had gone. A moth flew past like a ghost. Dilke entered his chamber and ate, then lay down and went quickly to sleep.

* * *

The night's growth had raised the orchid to the level of another briar. Dilke lay again at the entrance to the flower, stretched full length in the narrow tunnel.

He saw a sapsucker bug walk out on to the briar stem, a score or so micro-feet away, to feed in the warmth of the early sunlight. He saw a movement in the shadows at the end of the bridge. A round-bodied, shaggy creature crept from the jungle of leaves, moved on eight hairy legs towards the placid bug, and then, when it was within striking distance, leapt on to its back. Dilke watched breathlessly. It was like the attack of a tiger on a feeding buffalo, but the effect was more startlingly immediate. The bug died in an instant. The spider's teeth pierced its victim's neck and venom spurted from the hollow fangs into the cervical ganglia. The insect died without convulsion or struggle of any kind. For a minute victim and killer remained locked together then the spider withdrew its fangs and reinserted them further down the insect's back.

Dilke's eyes moved from the motionless creatures to the activities of other insects.

Butterflies unrolled their suction-hose tongues to probe into flowers for nectar, and continued their begetting and egg-laying as briskly as they had the previous day. An egg-layer, with flamboyant scarlet and purple wings folded, steadily traversed a leaf. A pigmy calcid wasp pursued her and deftly planted a parasitic egg in each newlaid shining globe, tiny germs of life which would become wasp grubs and feed on the infant caterpillars.

A large parasitic wasp landed on a leaf beside a fully grown caterpillar and used a more brutally direct way than its small cousin to provide her offspring with fresh meat. The caterpillar jerked up its tail and revealed two black spots like glaring eyes. Undeterred by this attempted intimidation, the wasp lanced her sting deep into her victim's body. Then, clutching her bulky prey, she lifted-off from the leaf and flew laboriously to the nest – larder and nursery combined – which she had prepared. The caterpillar was not dead. Dilke thought of its fate with a shudder of disgust. The wasp would wall-up the nest after laying eggs on the paralysed creature; the eggs would hatch and the larvae would eat the living caterpillar. Guided by an uncanny inherited knowledge they would feed in such a way that the caterpillar would remain alive until almost completely devoured.

While the jungle moved and buzzed with life all around, the spider continued its silent feast on the dead bug, growing more grossly corpulent as the day passed.

A deep, throbbing sound cut through the drone of insects. Dilke saw a flash of colour. The sound grew louder and a Cuban humming-bird waltzed down a sun-flecked avenue of leaves and shot out into the open valley. The bird darted to and fro; picked one, two, three gnats out of the air then vanished, leaving Dilke dazed by its sudden appearance and disappearance.

The bird came again, hurtling from the sky like a jet of liquid fire and jerked to a halt in mid-air.

The smallest bird on earth was a living helicopter to Dilke. A machine with an incredible hundred wing beats per second, which could hang in the air, could accelerate to seventy miles an hour, and fly backwards and forwards with equal facility.

It was so close that Dilke could see every detail: the long, narrow beak (the bird was two inches long, half of which was beak); the tucked-up legs and claws like a retracted undercarriage; the iridescent breast feathers covering the massive flight muscles, which gleamed with metallic blues and greens, and changed colour as the bird turned slowly in the air.

It turned until it faced Dilke from only inches away. The beak, stained with gnats' blood, was aimed point blank at the entrance to his refuge. It moved smoothly towards him; wind and noise from the blurred wings almost blinded and deafened him; he scrambled back and rolled into the belly of the flower.

The beak followed him into the orchid, passed over his head, and probed the back of the chamber. The wall gave way slightly under pressure; the beak drew back then rammed forward. A smell of penetrating sweetness filled Dilke's nostrils. The bird had pierced the wall and tapped the orchid's reservoir of nectar and was refuelling on the wing. Dilke heard the pulse of liquid in the long pipe-line of its hollow tongue. The whole flower shook in the wind from its beating wings, grains of pollen fell and adhered to the vibrating beak. Then the flow of nectar stopped and the beak was withdrawn and disappeared down the tunnel. The booming wingbeats increased to a roar as the bird accelerated away.

Dilke remained lying in the orchid after drinking from his new-found well. Within an hour he had visitors.

Attracted by the scent of nectar some small flying beetles entered the chamber. Folding their wings under lobster-red wing-cases, they ran to the hole made by the humming bird and supped the overflowing syrup.

Dilke examined them cautiously for fangs or claws before seizing one. He broke its neck with an oblique chopping blow behind the head with the hard edge of his right hand; then he twisted off its limbs and enjoyed a meal of the firm, white meat which he extracted from the hollow leg-casings.

Nectar and pollen followed.

He lay back and belched happily and scratched at the edges of the burn on his arm. The wound was healing, new skin formed a pink scar. He looked down at his naked body, tanned brown by exposure to the sun. He had reverted to his true scale of life in which insects were to be either preyed upon or feared as predators, but encircling his wrist was a link with the giant world of normal human society; of science and technology, politics and government, of war and pestilence, of espionage.

He stared at the wrist-watch: it was Friday, February 24th. Four minutes past seven; almost exactly six days since Cabral had taken them to La Club Americana.

For the first time since Gilbert Bellamy's death Dilke's thoughts returned to the events leading to the disastrous end of their mission.

What had made Lippe suspicious? Did he know about the mission in advance or had he discovered it since their arrival? Dilke could think of nothing which might have given them away; and yet – Dilke frowned – he felt that a clue to Lippe's knowledge lay just beyond his powers of recall.

And did Lippe's belief that they were *industrial* spies show that he was not involved in bacteriological weapon-making? Had the investigation been pointless? Had Bellamy died a futile death?

The beetles no longer drank at the well; a few had found concealment in the cluster of pollen grains and the rest had left the flower.

Dilke heard the whisper of his watch in the darkness and brought it to his ear. Bellamy's great watch with which it had kept time was now silent on the lake bottom around the fleshless bones of his killer's wrist.

The engine which had driven Bellamy's huge body was also silent.

With sudden insight Dilke saw that the days of shock and panic which followed the death of his companion were caused as much by the loss of that great heartbeat as from the real dangers he had experienced. He had been carried effortlessly and majestically through space, had shared the slow rhythm of Bellamy's breathing and the pulse of his blood – elemental as the flow of tides and the fall of waves – and he had felt invulnerable. How false that feeling had been! Gilbert Bellamy's death had ended an intimacy of thought and feeling which had been strangely intensified by the extreme difference in their statures.

Dilke scowled.

Even if the espionage had been misconceived; even if Compañía Peruana de Plásticos was innocent of arms trafficking; even if Lippe's grievance was sincere – the murder of Bellamy, the manner of his death, had been savage beyond reason.

Passionate hatred for the man who had caused it changed to sick rage as Dilke saw that he was impotent to revenge himself on Lippe. He swore vehemently and obscenely into the dark.

Dilke relived the events by the pigsty on the road to Lima. Projected on the curtain of his memory was the flashing knife in the half-breed's hand. Shirt and skin gave an instant's resistance before the blade plunged into the great belly. He saw bloody hands and a stricken face. Bellamy had wept at the imminence of death.

And he saw the raging piranhas and the repulsive half-breed's silent scream as he went down into his blood-bath. Dilke fell asleep, his face set in a mask of bitter satisfaction.

10

Dilke lay on the petal and leaned far out over its edge. The orchid blooms below made overlapping platforms leading down to the briar on which the spider had killed the sapsucker bug. It was a long drop to the first bloom, but he lowered himself over the edge of the petal without hesitation and let go. His fall was cushioned by the resilience of the platform; he dropped on to a third bloom then made a flying leap on to the briar.

The plant had a thicker stem with a rougher, harder, darker surface than the one on which he had first travelled; a soaring highway, studded at intervals with massive blood-red thorns like tank barriers.

Dilke's days as a disinterested observer of insect life were over; from his scented refuge in the orchid the behaviour of gaudy butterflies and savage wasps had seemed equally remote. Now he was back in the real world, but though he still feared its dangers he had learned that most insects were harmless. As in the larger world of mammals, herbivores vastly outnumbered predators. And many killers, like hunting wasps, were narrow specialists who were no threat to him, despite their strength and ferocity.

The predators Dilke feared were such freelance killers as spiders and assassin bugs, the lions and leopards of his microscopic world. Yet even they were programmed creatures, and against their instincts he could use logic. He could remain motionless before those who recognized only moving prey, and dive for cover from those who did not pursue victims which suddenly disappeared.

Dilke stepped forward. The journey which had been a mindless flight from danger now had a purpose.

His feelings towards Lippe had changed subtly overnight. Hatred remained, though in a less tempestuous form, but his thirst for revenge had grown stronger in spite of his powerlessness to satisfy it. Beyond the jungle stood a wall which marked the edge of Lippe's domain. Dilke was drawn on by a desire to be close to, to see, to observe, to study, and *somehow* to injure Professor Heinrich Lippe.

The spider's victim was still on the briar, attached to the surface by its beak. It had only two wounds: a double incision in the neck through which venom and a liquidizing enzyme had been injected; and another in the body from which the organs and muscles had been sucked after being reduced to soup. The body was now a collapsed bag of leather which smelled faintly putrid.

Farther on Dilke found the remains of another sapsucker. The body had disappeared, leaving the head and beak standing at a drunken angle like an abandoned road drill. It was bleached and dried-out by the tropical sun and rattled when he lifted it. He examined it with curiosity, then banged it on the briar until the head and long beak broke apart. Then he smashed the beak against a thorn until it split to reveal the internal mechanism — a suction tube between two piercing blades. With growing excitement he extracted the shrunken tube and shook out the blades. They were long, tapered and slightly curved across their widths; they had sharp points and edges, and stubs which had fitted into the beast's head. He seized one and struck joyfully at the thorn. Dehydration had made the blade heavy and hard, a chunk of wood flew up and fell into the chasm.

He had found a primitive weapon; though useless against a large insect, he could use it against smaller ones; and while it increased his chance of survival only slightly its possession elated him.

The handle was too rough, so he bound it with a length of shining silk web (relic of a young spider's descent from the sky) which he found caught on the briar. He knotted silk cord into a harness and slung the sword across his back with its hilt jutting above his shoulder, samurai fashion. Then he coiled the remaining cord around his waist and strode up the road into a landscape of leaves.

A multitude of insects pastured on the suspended leaf-green fields. He climbed on to a leaf where a score of sapsuckers browsed, and attacked a straggler. Emulating the spider he plunged his sword into the bug's neck but it did not die instantly; it went into convulsions and rolled off the leaf, almost taking the sword with it.

Dilke tried again; he faced a half-grown bug, stabbed over its lowered head, and before the stricken beast could withdraw its sucker, he dropped all his weight on its head to pin it down; its death struggles went unheeded by its placidly feeding neighbours. He opened its gut and drank the sweet contents, then carried off its head and a haunch of meat.

Dilke had a plan: after eating, he broke off the insect's beak, then levered it open with his sword-point and extracted a blade. A short, broad blade, still sticky with sap, which would harden as it dried out – a knife to go with the heavy sword.

The tangled briars made a network of arterial roads through the forest; when those on which he travelled swung away from the wall he changed to others which took him towards it. To gain height more rapidly, he sometimes left the roads and ascended bamboo stems.

He slept wherever he could find concealment; the junction of a leaf and stem, the cup of a flower, the hollow carcase of a long-dead spider. Late one afternoon he came upon a batch of insect eggs as big as wine casks; he climbed into an empty egg and used the remaining hours of daylight to weave an all-purpose net; a hammock, provisions-carrier and catch-net for small insects.

He had put aside the net and curled up to sleep when the rumble of distant voices made him instantly alert. The voices grew louder and more distinct, speaking an unintelligible Spanish/Indian patois punctuated with harsh laughter and accompanied by the clatter of giant feet on the metal ramp. A blaze of light suddenly illuminated the thicket. There were shouts, the sounds of a struggle, and of splashing water, but nothing was visible through the dense foliage.

The light went out. Dilke stared over the rim of the egg into darkness and listened to the fading noises of departure; then he lay down to sleep.

The sound of caterpillars hatching awakened Dilke. He watched them squirm out of the rows of eggs and hump their way across the leaf to feed on its outer edge. He heard the jaws of a neighbour crunching into its prison wall, and he killed the creature as it escaped. Its green-and-black hide bristled with hairs like a hog, and its flesh was tough and unappetizing. He breakfasted on a residue of yolk in the bottom of the egg then climbed down on to the highway.

Dilke had developed a degree of fatalism towards the hazards of his situation; though sharply aware of his surroundings he no longer constantly looked over his shoulder for imagined dangers.

A low buzz of awakening forest life filled the air. He walked in the morning light and wondered over the things he had heard in the night, and he thought with renewed curiosity about the purpose of the ramp and the chute which overhung the lake.

A gaily coloured leafhopper dropped on to the road ahead and sat up brightly to groom its feathery antennae. In the instant when Dilke halted at its appearance two jointed limbs flashed out and snatched the hopper from the briar. The sudden movement revealed a green mantis, three inches high, which had struck from ambush with lightning speed. It was a monster of legendary ferocity of which he had heard but never seen. He stared at its spread wings and slim body as it crushed the hopper in the angles of its powerful spiked forelimbs. It bent its long neck and, disregarding the struggles of its screeching victim, began to eat with fastidious neatness. Dilke stood irresolutely and watched blood from the dying hopper spatter on to the road. Was it safe to pass? The mantis was preoccupied; as Dilke stepped forward he saw a flash of green wings further up the road as a second mantis struck.

Dilke returned to an offshoot from the main stem and took this side road.

The leaves were thinning out and the pervading light had lost its green, aquatic quality. He had almost reached the upper limits of the forest and could see patches of sky and glimpse parts of the huge concrete barrier.

A few hours brought him clear. He climbed on to a high leaf and walked around its perimeter to look across the roof of the forest. The intricate and shadowy world of leaf and branch through which he had climbed for seven days was below; the steel and wooden structure from which the sound of human voices had come was to the south. To the north was the wall – crowned with a tangle of barbed wire and living thorn.

His arrival on the wall coincided with sunset. The surface of the terrace, a vast desert two thousand micro-feet below, was in shadow. He shielded his eyes against the red sun, mirrored in the distant office windows.

A man stood in the middle of the terrace by the statue of the horse.

Mathew Dilke's heart lurched.

It was Lippe.

He had one hand on the shoulder of the gaunt beast and held a small book, with his forefinger inserted as placemarker, against his breast with the other. The sun was going down fast; Lippe sank into a quick-sand of shadow; at last only his disembodied head remained, bathed in red, calmly watching the spectacular conflagration of clouds over the distant Pacific.

The light faded; a figure crossed the faintly illumin-ated study window, the motor which opened and closed the glass door to the study purred twice, then there was silence.

Moonlight revealed a shallow crack in the top of the wall. Dilke climbed into its shelter and examined new feelings which stirred within him.

Coming upon Lippe so suddenly had carried him across a psychological threshold between the micro-world of insects and the world of man. And he discovered, to his surprise, that seeing Lippe had not inflamed his hatred of him; the passionate sun of hate had been followed, inexplicably, by a cold moon of intellectual curiosity.

What was Lippe? A biochemist, a businessman, a connoisseur – a vindictive and murderous old man. Dilke's thoughts ran back when he closed his eyes, tracing the events which followed his arrival in Lima, returning again and again to the enigma of Lippe's personality.

He lay back and stared at the night sky. The moon above had shone down on England only hours before. The idea brought no comfort, but only intensified his feelings of desperate and brutal isolation.

Dilke set off at first light, climbing down into the vast curtain of foliage which hung from the top of the wall to the terrace far below. Dropping on his rope from leaf to leaf, his descent was so rapid that he almost completed the climb in a day.

At ten next morning he stood at the edge of the glaring white desert and squinted at the far-off building. The sun was already unbearably hot and he decided to wait till after midday before starting his trek; he could travel by moonlight if necessary. He retreated to the shadows at the foot of the wall and took meat from his net and began to eat, seizing it between his teeth and slicing off mouthfuls with his knife. Rising currents of air from the hot plastic surface of the desert stirred the leaves which surrounded him, leaning them over like a fleet of great sails in a breeze.

Two leaves, joined together on a single stalk, turned in a strangely contrary way. Icy fear seized Dilke. The leaves were green wings!

Two pairs of articulated legs supported the stalklike body from which the wings sprouted. A neat triangular head with huge globular eyes and horny jaws surmounted the long neck. Cousin to the elegant butcher which had killed the leafhopper, its spiked forearms were folded back in the characteristic attitude which had earned it the name *Mantis religiosa* – the praying mantis.

The monster leaned towards him and its massive arms jerked like a mechanical grab just put into gear.

Dilke crouched in the open desert and spat out a mouthful of meat. He found to his dazed surprise that he held a slab of meat in one hand and his knife in the other; he had no recollection of running from the mantis; he threw down the meat and stared fearfully under the leaves, then moved along the edge of the jungle peering into the shadows. He could see nothing. But there might be a whole colony of the bastards in there!

He remembered, with a shudder, the insect's bulging green eyes with their pinpoint pupils fixed on him. He turned away from the jungle; sun or no sun he would not return to it now.

From the wall the terrace had seemed quite flat, but from ground level he could see shallow undulations stretching to the horizon.

The dryness of his lips anticipated the thirst to come. He tightened his sword harness, secured the carry-net and climbing rope at his waist and stepped forward grimly. The sculpted horse was a landmark throwing a long shadow towards him which grew shorter as the sun climbed higher. As he hurried to reach this promised relief from heat and glare it receded before him. He quickened his pace, trotting in pursuit of the shadow, but gave up at last to sit exhausted on a slope and watch it fly away.

He fixed his eyes on the horse and doggedly recommenced his journey.

At midday he walked under a hoof as big as the Albert Hall and collapsed in its shade.

Half-blinded by travelling through shimmering light and miniature sandstorms of fine plastic dust he lay with closed eyes until the residual flashes and stars of light had faded from his eyelids.

The underside of the hoof was not sprayed with white plastic like its exterior; reflected light from the surrounding desert revealed that the great arched surface was dark and rough, and Dilke saw that it had been accurately modelled, even a horseshoe was carved round the outer edge.

He examined the hoof more carefully. A forest of black hair grew from its heel, spattered with gobs of white plastic. He looked up with wonder at huge, metal nail-heads in a rust-red shoe and recognized the acrid smells of hoof-horn and stable-muck which filled the air.

After lying beneath the hoof for an hour he set off again, and as he walked away in the shadow of the great plastic-coated carcass he looked back. It stood silhouetted against the western sky with sunlight streaming through the ligaments which bound its enormous rib-cage.

The beast was *not* by Dali out of Hepworth!

Dilke trudged on. Was it a monument, a folly, a joke? It might even be a *sort* of work of art – or a clue to the mystery of its owner's soul.

PART FOUR

11

Dilke waited outside the closed door to Lippe's office. The sun, which was far to the west, had lost its power but the ground retained its heat. The huge door of glass and steel fitted so exactly into the grooved threshold that he had been unable to enter the building. Dilke ran his dry tongue over parched lips. It was a situation he had not foreseen. What if Lippe stayed indoors? If the door remained shut he would be stranded, separated by desert from sources of food and water. And returning to the jungle would just put off the problem; he would then have to make the long journey back.

If the door opened he would have only seconds to enter. He dismissed his apprehensions and readied himself for action, standing tensely at the side from which it would open.

He heard the muffled sound of approaching footsteps. The motor growled and the door rolled back. A giant foot crashed down and Lippe walked out on to the terrace followed by a cool air-conditioned breeze.

An inch-deep metal channel, much too wide to jump, barred his way. Dust and grit, which had fallen into the trench and been pushed along by the door, made a pile of rubble at the end. Dilke dropped into the trench and scrambled up the slope. From the corner of his eye he saw the great door returning at express speed. Vibration and his flying feet loosened the rocks beneath him.

He would be crushed against the end of the trench.

Terror drove him to extraordinary feats of agility. He reached the top of the slope, leapt, grabbed the edge of the trench, jerked himself up and rolled on to the threshold. The door slammed shut.

He listened to the measured thud and creak of rope-soled slippers outside on the terrace and fought down the fear of what might have been. It was a long time before he felt steady enough to continue.

The floor before him was as waterless as the terrace; he had moved from a white into a black wasteland. He must find food and water. The Aid contained both. Though it might be anywhere in the room – or have been destroyed – his instinct told him that he would find it on the desk.

In fifteen minutes he had passed the television console and reached a long table adjoining the desk; the trestle legs were climbable but the table top overlapped them, making it impossible to reach its upper surface.

Lippe's leather and stainless steel chair had a central column supported on a tripod. The column was threaded like a bolt to permit the height of the seat to be adjusted. Dilke traced a route along a tripod leg with his eyes, then up the ridges of the threaded column and into the metal shell of the chair. From its interior there might be a way out on to an arm, and from there a way on to the desk. But he found that the gap between chair and desk was too wide to cross.

The glint of a hinged cover to a floor socket caught

his eye; three massive cables rose from it; Dilke hurried towards them. A lamp flex and two telephone cables which hung down from the desk were plugged into the sunken junction box. The flex was unclimbable, but the cables ascended in tight curls for a thousand micro-feet; like spiral stairways.

He stepped on to one and started the long climb, rushing it too much as he had on the briar by the lake. He had lost a lot of water since morning and halfway up the cable he was so exhausted, and dizzy from turning interminably to the right that he lay down and closed his eyes. Dilke knew the facts about dying from thirst: dizziness, headaches, nausea, a swollen tongue, stiff limbs and – long before death – final immobility. Without food a man could survive for weeks but, in Dilke's gruelling circumstances, he could live for only days without water.

He opened dull eyes and saw Lippe through the window, slowly pacing the terrace and reading a book in the pink evening light.

Dilke forced his aching body on. The dryness had spread from his nose and mouth into his windpipe and gullet. His former optimism he now saw had come from wishful thinking. Even if the Aid was on the desk it could be anywhere among the acres of books, or buried under papers.

At last he crawled up the final few millimetres of cable, tumbled on to the edge of the desk and staggered round corner of the telephone. The lamplight almost blinded him. Standing in the shadow of a porcelain tobacco jar – between a bottle of pills and a box of matches – was the Aid.

Dilke gave a croak of incredulous joy and crossed the desk to the Aid. He clawed his way up the ladder, lurched into the shower bay and stood open-mouthed under the streaming water. He drank till he could drink no more then threw off his sword and harness and sat under the shower and drank again. Leaving wet footprints, he went to the food store and wolfed a meal. He returned to the bathroom with Scotch and a glass and lay in the overflowing bathtub with closed eyes, drinking slowly, rapturously holding the whisky in his mouth before swallowing it. The water seemed to soak into his bones and a dreamlike feeling of well-being possessed him.

At last he rose and shaved. He looked into his hollow eyes and saw what thirteen days in the wilderness had done: his face was thinner, his body leaner and harder and burnt brown by sun and wind. He put on a clean cat-suit – relishing the feel of cloth on skin – and climbed to the upper floor with the bottle and glass. The transparent dome had been removed, it lay on the desk below him and the detachable 'map pin' observation satellite lay beside it.

Lippe's huge mottled hand moved across the desk a yard away, writing with a pen like Nelson's Column on a pad as big as Trafalgar Square.

Dilke's drinking began as a celebration, but somewhere along the road to total drunkenness his Scotch-induced euphoria changed to morose introspection. He recalled the purpose of his visit to Peru, and his doubts about Lippe's complicity in making biological weapons faded before the feeling – it was no more than an intuition – that the head of C.P.P. was engaged in something less innocent than the making of plastics.

By midnight, when he finished the bottle, he had decided. He remembered Bellamy. He would continue the investigation they had begun together. He would start tomorrow with the room behind the hessian door through which Schmidt had made his brief appearance.

The alarm went off like a rattlesnake and Dilke groaned at his thudding headache. He lay and waited till the reverberations faded and he cursed himself: he could not face the journey to Schmidt's room with this crushing hangover. He sat up shakily on the bunk and squinted at a sheet of notepaper stuck to the wall. There was writing on the paper. 'For all guilt is punished on earth!' He dimly remembered scrawling it before falling into bed. It was a proclamation of intent – a piece of drunken irony – he would make Lippe feel the weight of Goethe's words! Now the whisky-bravado was gone, replaced by self-disgust. He remembered with alarm that he had sat in the observation chair with the trap-door open and with the Aid's lights on; his flesh crawled at the thought of what might have followed if Lippe had seen the light. Retrospective fear was followed by fear of present dis-covery and recapture; Dilke crept from the Aid to find a safer place of concealment.

There was a recess in the pipe-rack but the stink from the row of great pipes turned his stomach.

There was access to the inside of a phone through holes in its base but if it rang his head would explode!

He found a way into a mahogany desk calendar with an interior as high and as dimly lit as a church. Narrow beams of light illuminated the crude wooden cogs and huge rollers which moved the bands of letters and num-bers.

By afternoon the worst of his hangover had passed, leaving a foul taste in his mouth and a sensation of shivery lightheadedness. He climbed up on to the lowest roller and peered out of the aperture through which the numerals were visible.

Lippe sat with his elbows on the desk, his pipe glowing like Vesuvius and his hooded eyes gazing into space.

Dilke realized that he had panicked; if he showed no lights in the Aid he should be safe in it.

He left the calendar and returned to the Aid, where he ate a light supper and went early to bed.

The room and its furniture were as functional as an operating theatre, but a wall of leather-bound books and another of framed drawings and paintings softened its austerity.

Dilke stood at the top of the steps in the Aid with only his head above the trapdoor in the observation platform.

A man's possessions reveal his character: Dilke gave Lippe's room a long and patient examination. Though plastics were Lippe's business he evidently did not share his sales manager's passion for them: his chair was steel and leather, his desk top a sheet of black glass, his walls were covered in golden-brown hessian; only the floor was plastic.

Evidence of the professor's industry lay on the desk and overflowed on to the long and incongruously make-shift trestle table which stood beside it. Books and journals were piled up like city blocks, with dust and spent matches and shreds of tobacco littering the avenues between them. Beyond the stacked books towered sky-scraper boxfiles and high jars of rock-like crystals.

The Aid was only one of many objects crowded around a desk writing set; there was a stapler, a paper knife, scattered paper-clips, a jar full of pencils and biros, and a dead bluebottle.

But nothing he saw told Dilke more than he already knew; that Heinrich Lippe was cultured, industrious, prosperous, and not addicted to tidiness.

The old man worked at his desk all day then closed his books, refilled and lit his pipe, and went out on to the terrace.

Dilke started his journey of exploration with the zipped pockets of his jacket filled with gear: torch, camera, binoculars, recorder; and – with the terrors of defencelessness fresh in his mind – loaded with grenades and a crossbow. He had descended only part of the way down the spiralling phone cable when the strip of light which shone beneath the hessian-covered door went out. Schmidt entered the room then made an exit into the corridor, leaving a line of faint footprints behind on the smooth surface of the floor, and the same elusive smell which had accompanied his brief entry into the room during Bellamy's visit to Lippe.

Dilke got down to the floor and in twenty minutes reached the perimeter of a footprint. The dust left by the sole of the German's enormous shoe was not, he discovered, grains of powder but ragged blocks of sawdust and fragments of bran.

He passed under the door into a crimson twilight, and as his eyes adjusted to the darkness he saw that he had entered a narrow, windowless room lit by a single red bulb. On his left, a long bench ran the whole length of the room, with the tops of laboratory hardware just visible over its edge. On his right there were wire-fronted cages from floor to ceiling. Far away, at the end of the narrow space between bench and cages, a refrigerator purred faintly.

The bench front was as smooth as an ice cliff.

If he was to see the lab equipment he would have to view it from the wall of cages opposite. He headed for the cages across a floor strewn with sawdust and bran, mixed with smooth brown boulders and jagged lumps of crystal, their facets glowing like fire.

Dilke froze as he heard a scuffle from the shadows, then stepped behind a boulder as an insect, shaped like a shallow upturned boat, scuttled out of a crack beneath a cage. Lightly touching bran and sawdust with its whip-lash antenna as it passed, it stopped at a boulder like the one which concealed Dilke. It was a big tropical cockroach an inch and a half long. After exploring the surface of the boulder with its antenna it lifted it in its spiny forelimbs and rattled away on its four rear legs.

Dilke shot it before it reached its den.

It was the unprovoked killing of a harmless scavenger, a celebration of his newly acquired fire-power. The percussion head of the crossbow bolt blasted a hole in the beast's carapace and the hollow shaft burst inside it, shooting venom into its abdomen. He examined the dead cockroach with satisfaction and found that the massive boulder which it still clutched was not the rock it appeared; the hard, brown crust had broken, revealing a soft interior. It was a mousedropping. Dilke pulled a face; now he had the ingredients of the perplexing smell: dung, crystals and sawdust, the odours of pet shop and chemical lab combined.

He came to the cages and laboriously climbed their quarter-inch wire mesh fronts, resting at each tier of cages and seeing more and more equipment as he ascended. Halfway up a cage front on the third tier he came level with the bench top and stared across the wide canyon at an array of metal and glass which shone in the crimson light like a vast industrial complex seen from half a mile away. Microscopes, chemical balances, a spectroscope and row upon row of glass containers, but nothing which resembled the centrifuges or temperature-control drums or racks of germ-incubation flasks he had seen at Porton. He would have liked to record it all but it was too dark for camera work.

Papers hung on clips from the wall; he trained field glasses on them and tried, unsuccessfully, to read them.

The contents of the jars might be significant; Dilke recalled that a description of germ culture in his files gave recipes for culture solutions ...

He ran the glasses slowly along the labelled containers; Schmidt's bold hand was clear enough even at this distance. Most of the names were of simple basic chemicals which he committed to memory, the rest he dictated into his pocket recorder:

'Ferrous fumerate and ferrous gluconate; pempidine tartrate; Ephedrine; Frat 1 and Frat 2 ...'

He heard a movement in the cage behind him. A huge twitching nose issued from a strawstack in the corner; a beast crawled from the nest and scuffled to a bowl of water, then made an excursion round the edges of the cage. It was a white mouse turned pink, with protruding eyes turned purple, and yellow tombstone teeth turned as red as blood by the laboratory night-light.

It paused just below Dilke's perch on the netting to scratch itself, then sat up to give its whiskers a vigorous grooming. It was a female in an advanced stage of pregnancy, her enormous belly smeared with milk from her swollen dugs. She dropped on to all fours and returned to the nest, ploughing a wide furrow in the sawdust litter and leaving a pungent odour in Dilke's nostrils.

He moved across the front of the mouse's cage and came to a large glass-fronted container like an empty aquarium or a cage for reptiles. It contained no litter, but there were tufts of fur on the floor and streaks of dried and flaking liquid on the inner surface of the glass; streaks as black as tar in the ruby light. 'Blood,' muttered Dilke, and stared into the darkness at the back of the cage. Perhaps a snake lay in the shadow. Despite the plate glass which stood between him and the cage's interior he felt threatened by an imagined presence. His eyes, strained by his efforts to pierce the gloom, saw shifting, dissolving shapes. The hair lifted on his scalp. All around him the rustling of a myriad caged creatures underlaid the hum from the refrigerator, and their movements were transmitted to the ledge beneath his feet.

The whole room seemed to watch and wait; across the chasm between cages and bench the glassware glinted with an inexplicable silent menace.

Dilke descended the huge climbing-frames of netting and hurried across the laboratory floor and out under the door.

12

As he waited at his observation post in the morning for the arrival of the professor, Dilke's old doubts about Lippe's culpability returned. Perhaps the secret lab work was on plastic after all; none of the chemicals which Dilke had listed were mentioned in the germ-culture file. He had checked when he got back to the Aid the previous night and double-checked after breakfast. Dilke's mouth twisted wryly. But plastics and pet shops did not mix!

Lippe arrived at nine and swung his chair round until only its back was visible to Dilke. There was a click, followed by the fizz of a television set warming up and the creak of leather as the old man sat down. The sounds of voices and machinery suddenly became audible, changing abruptly in character and volume as Lippe switched from station to station; then a second click brought silence and Lippe swung round to his desk and made notes on a pad.

Dilke's view of the television had been obscured by the great curved wall of Lippe's chair and the old man's writing was not visible from Dilke's position on the desk.

Dilke swore softly and impatiently at the restricted viewpoint imposed on him by his place in the Aid.

Lippe rang Schmidt on the intercom at intervals during the morning, and around midday Lippe received a call from his assistant. Schmidt's voice was inaudible to Dilke but the old man echoed some of his words: 'Botticelli ... Kirangozi ... Makhov ... Bodovsky ... Saturday ...'

Lippe replaced the receiver, picked up a pen and drew his desk diary towards him. Before pen touched paper Dilke was on his way down the steps to his files. His lips moved soundlessly as he pulled open a drawer and hunted through the files. Bodovsky, Bodovsky, Bodovsky.

He plucked out the *Who's Who* folder and ran a finger down the list: Bodovsky followed Bodell, James; who was preceded by Bellamy, Gilbert.

Bodovsky, Eugene. Colonel, U.S.S.R. Army Intelligence. Accompanied Russian Trade Delegation as a civilian when it visited Peru last October. Visited Compañía Peruana de Plásticos during that time.

Makhov was not listed, nor were the other names.

Dilke slammed the file shut and returned to his post to find Lippe gone and the diary lying open only a few inches from the Aid. But Lippe's writing, seen upside-down, was made totally unreadable by the extreme perspective of the page; try as he might Dilke could not decipher it. He glanced at his watch. Twelve forty-five, time for Lippe's midday meal; on an impulse Dilke left the Aid and ran out on to the glassy surface of the desk. He climbed the splayed pages of the diary and hurried across the open page to the writing which had not quite dried. Ink crept almost imperceptibly along the tangled white fibres and the pen-strokes faded slightly as the ink soaked into the mat of paper.

Lippe's cramped hand was as big as beach-writing to Dilke. He walked slowly from letter to huge letter, spelling out and memorizing the words, then he returned to the Aid at a run and wrote down what he had seen:

Saturday
2.30 F R A T. Botticelli, Kirangozi, Makhov, Bodovsky.

Unless Botticelli was a dead painter, Lippe was to have a meeting with four people in five days' time.

About what? About F R A T?

Dilke sat on the side of his bunk and scowled with concentration. A small voice deep down inside told him that Saturday at two-thirty would be a day and a time of great significance. But F R A T conveyed nothing to him, neither as a word nor as the initials to four words.

Dilke snatched a meal and returned to his stand at the top of the ladder. As he watched Lippe he grew increasingly dissatisfied with what he could see from the Aid, and frustrated by hearing only half of what passed over the telephone.

By mid-afternoon he decided to move.

He descended to his quarters and prepared himself, putting on the big, belted jacket and filling its capacious pockets with the camera and the other items he had taken on his trip to the lab. He packed a rucksack with supplies, and a bedroll, and his silk climbing rope; he armed himself fully and, taking the telephone line-tapper with him, surreptitiously left the Aid.

Before leaving the desk he climbed into the dark interior of Lippe's telephone through a ventilation hole in its base. There he attached the line-tapper and plugged the recorder into it. There was enough tape to record six hours of speech, and as the tape would run only when activated by sound it was more than enough.

He descended the spiralling cable to the floor and waited by the great square column of a desk leg until the old man left the room for his customary stroll on the terrace.

Then Dilke ran beneath the chair, mounted a tripod leg, travelled along its one-in-two slope to the threaded central column and climbed up towards the dark underside of the chair seat. It was more difficult than he had bargained for. Even though it was an ascent of only three hundred micro-feet the space between each projecting thread was just too wide to make climbing easy. He grunted up the last inch of column, struggled on to the horizontal flange of a massive L-shaped girder and threw down his rucksack; then he undid his jacket with trembling fingers and sat back against the girder wall to cool off.

The frame of the chair was steel, cushioned with foam rubber and covered with leather.

Dilke was on the main beam which ran beneath the seat from front to back and then rose vertically to support the chair-back. The foam cushion above him rested on a square mesh of metal; the mesh rested on, and was welded to, the chassis of the chair.

The sound of the door to the terrace sliding open brought him to his feet. Lippe was on his way back. Dilke looked around wildly for a place of security, a refuge against the chair's inevitably violent movements when Lippe sat down.

Twenty paces along the girder he saw the countersunk head of a metal screw, but before he could reach the shelter of the slot in its head an unseen hand spun the chair and he was flung against the metal wall.

When Heinrich Lippe's vast bulk descended, hurricane and earthquake combined.

Dilke lay in the angle of the girder and heard an ear-splitting squeal of leather and the roar of wind expelled from the foam-rubber cushion.

A hail of dust and foam particles was discharged from the honeycombed interior of the cushion as it was squeezed down on to the steel grid, and Dilke felt the metal beneath him shudder and groan as Lippe's full weight settled into the chair.

When the storm subsided Dilke scrambled on all fours along the girder and tumbled into the slot in the screw-head.

He was in a narrow trench (the size of a coffin, he thought grimly) and safe from sudden movements. He spread his bedroll beneath him and reconciled himself to staying there until the chair was vacated. The rotation of the chair had thrown him against the wall but he might not be as lucky next time; if he was standing and the chair swung the other way he would be thrown off the girder.

The steel bars twanged sonorously overhead; he lay on his back and watched the ceiling of grey bulges expand and contract through the mesh as Lippe shifted ponderously in his seat.

Dilke's plan was to climb to the very highest point on the chair, for when Lippe had turned it round to watch television Dilke had seen a way to the top – a zip-fastener ran all the way up the back of the chair like a huge metal ladder.

He fell asleep before the old man retired for the

night, then was wakened momentarily by the sudden stillness after Lippe left the chair.

Dilke woke and ate and packed his gear by torchlight, then set off along the dim metal causeway towards the zip-fastener.

Getting on to the inner side of the zip was simple enough, but climbing down, then under, then up on to the outside of the huge metal teeth was a lot less easy. It took him an hour and it was six o'clock before he started the long, long climb. There were three hours left before Lippe's arrival.

The edges of the chair-cover slightly overlapped the zip, making a narrow crevice on each side of the fastener into which he squeezed when he needed rest.

He reached the top with half-an-hour in hand; he climbed over the leather piping which terminated the fastener and stood breathlessly on the ridge. The great curved wings of the chair lay to north and south. Dilke hurried to the left and jogged along the top of the ridge with a sheer drop to the chair seat on one side and the low parapet of piping on the other.

The view from the end of the ridge was tremendous. The half-circle of the chair back – like a sweep of smooth basalt rock – enclosed a vast and shadowy bay. To Dilke, the eastern wing of the chair was quarter of a mile away and the floor, seen over the steep down-curve of the wing on which he stood, was a dizzy one thousand and five hundred micro-feet below.

He searched without success for a fold or a split or crevice in the smooth surface of the leather into which he could crawl.

He glanced at his watch, then quickly fitted a bolt into his crossbow, stood back from the leather pipeline, and

138

fired into it. The explosive head of the bolt blew a hole as big as his head in the side of the pipe. He dropped a grenade into the hole and ran along the ridge and crouched down. The sound of the explosion was followed by a single flat echo from across the bay. He ran back and swore joyfully at the effect of the explosion; the grenade had blown a seven micro-foot gap in the pipe – less than half-an-inch – too small to be noticed by the old man but entirely adequate for Dilke's purposes.

He waited until smoke from the open ends of the pipe had cleared, then he threw his pack into the hole, which gave him a view west towards Lippe's desk, and crawled in after it. The lingering grenade fumes slowly thinned leaving a smell of scorched leather. Dilke stared out through the tattered entrance of the tunnel and waited impatiently for Lippe's arrival.

13

Heinrich Lippe arrived at nine and turned his chair to face the television.

The swing of the chair threw Dilke against the curved wall of the tunnel. He rolled back amongst a tangle of bedding and tackle, then wriggled forward on his belly and looked out of his hiding-place.

From desk-level the professor's head had been like an effigy carved out of a distant mountain top.

Now Dilke was close enough to see every pore and wrinkle on the great face.

The head was like a massive block of eroded stone; time had hollowed the temples and ploughed a network of channels in the yellow-grey skin. A perfunctory shave had left stumps of hair on the mottled jowls; thickets of white hairs grew on the jutting brows and from the ears; a single hair sprouted from a mole on the long upper lip and trembled in the air which flowed intermittently from the cavernous nostrils.

The head of the colossus rested against the encircling chair back and his hands rested palms down on his thighs. Only the eyes in the impassive face showed expression. From beneath heavy lids they stared at the television images with the same steady concentration Dilke had noticed when Lippe had given his brief audience to Gilbert Bellamy.

Dilke recognized the picture on the screen – it was the fibreglass bonding section in the boat-building shed. Lippe switched to another part of the factory, and then to the warehouse. Switching alternately between the twin screens he completed his closed-circuit rounds of factory, labs and quarry in half an hour.

It was the start of a working day which did not finish until after midnight, and throughout the long hours Dilke watched everything which Lippe did and wrote.

The apparent dusty disorder which Dilke had seen from desk-level was revealed by his new and commanding viewpoint to be a superficial untidiness; for Lippe's folders, files and journals were arranged on his desk and table with obsessive orderliness.

And by the afternoon of the following day, Dilke realized that the pipe-smoking reveries, the daydreaming through the window which overlooked the sunlit lake, the reflective strolls on the terrace – all the manifestations of professorial vagueness and absent-mindedness – gave a totally wrong picture of Lippe's nature. For Lippe's days were rigidly programmed from the moment he entered the room at nine until he finally left it sixteen hours later. He spent the mornings on administration, and the afternoons on paperwork, filling pages with columns of complex mathematical equations. Then he read technical and management journals in the early part of the evening before returning again to his calculations.

Lippe ran Compañía Peruana de Plásticos through

Schmidt. He ran it autocratically and peremptorily, without a trace of the benevolence he had displayed during Bellamy's visit.

On the afternoon of Dilke's second day on the wing of the chair Lippe ended several hours of deep concentration on his figures by picking up his phone. 'I have finished the formula, Schmidt.'

Within minutes the German silently entered the room and disappeared through the laboratory door with a sheet of Lippe's scribbled hieroglyphics. The wail of the distant factory hooter drifted up the hillside; Lippe picked up the book which he often read on the terrace and left the room.

The light had faded when he returned. He switched on the desk light, but before he had seated himself Schmidt spoke to him from the laboratory doorway. The professor laid the book down and followed his assistant through the door.

The book lay at the centre of the circle of light. It was a slim red volume with gilded page-edges and soft leather covers; left open at the page which Lippe had been reading.

As Dilke watched, the pages turned as if moved by an invisible hand.

They moved slowly at first then more quickly, until the book lay flat and still. It was clear from the stained margins of its pages and its disposition to fall open at this place that its owner had returned here again and again.

Marquis de Sade: Reflections was printed in antique capitals at the head of the pages. Three heavily-drawn lines in the margin marked a paragraph: 'Nature averse to crime! I tell you nature lives and breathes by it, hungers at all her pores for bloodshed, yearns with all her heart for the furtherance of cruelty.'

Thirty words which embodied the whole philosophy of sadism (Dilke looked fixedly at them), and which opened the door a crack on Lippe's dark and secret mind.

Dilke knew the words by heart when the old man returned at last to his desk, and he looked with new insight into the great impassive face.

Lippe closed and put aside Sade's reflections and opened the day's financial and scientific magazines; he quickly disposed of finance and chemistry then sat back contentedly with a magazine on psychobiology.

He passed over articles on hallucinogens and on bird migration. He paused to study a picture of captive rabbits inhaling tobacco smoke in aid of cancer research. He read about the Russian transplant of a cat's head on to a dog's body, and he showed interest in the report of an American attempt to keep an isolated chimpanzee brain alive and functioning: the brain had lived for a week.

'Pain: its mechanism and manifestations,' a long article written by several research teams, filled the last half of the journal. 'Pain as an alarm signal; the route of pain from its source to the seat of sensation in the brain; the evolution of pain from a primitive diffused sensation to a sophisticated many-faceted one.' A Cleveland team had devised a series of experiments to discover the answers to three questions: are sensations of pain located in one part of the brain? Is pain from specific parts of the body registered in particular brain cells? Are different forms of pain (cutting, crushing, burning, and so on) registered in 'specialist' brain cells?

143

The monitoring of the electrical brain activity of laboratory rats undergoing stimulation had proved the existence of 'pain centres', but evidence for a relationship between specific pains and 'specialist' brain cells was disappointingly inconclusive. Lippe brooded over the paired illustrations of subjects undergoing various forms of painful stimulation and graphs of their electric brain patterns.

The Cleveland men had asked themselves a final question: does the maturity of a subject affect its sensitivity to pain?

A full-page coloured photograph illustrated one of a series of tests. An infant rat, enclosed in a glass cube, stood on a floor of close-set bars with wires trailing from two electrodes inserted in its skull. It stood upright, forearms outstretched, body and paws pressed against the glass. The bars on which it stood glowed red. Smoke from its charred hind feet filled the box. Its fur was criss-crossed by singe-marks. Its eyes were shut tight and a photoflash had frozen a split second of agony into an everlasting scream.

Dilke stared at the ugly, stumpy, pitiful creature and was turned to stone.

The magazine trembled in its reader's massive hands. Dilke turned his head stiffly and looked into Lippe's face. Breath wheezed unevenly through the man's parted lips and sweat lay in the folds of his parchment skin, his eyes had a fixed and vacant gaze.

Schmidt's entry into the room broke the spell.

Lippe's eyes came back into focus and he moved a hand in dismissal rather than acknowledgment of his assistant's 'Goodnight'.

When the German had gone his master began his evening's work, but first he carefully snipped out the picture of the rat and put it at the back of a thick journal which he took from a desk drawer.

Professor Lippe put away his work at midnight, then he filled a fresh pipe and lit it with deliberation before taking the journal from its drawer. He sat with the heavy volume against the desk and resting on his knees. From it he abstracted the magazine page and gazed at the photograph for a long moment before replacing it and turning to an earlier part of the book.

The pages were covered with writing. It was Lippe's personal journal, containing his thoughts on a multitude of topics.

The last entry was an equation to which Lippe had added a question mark; he gazed at it and gently tapped the page with the air of a crossword addict pondering over a tricky clue.

To Dilke, looking down from his hiding-place on the arm of the chair, the figures and symbols were incomprehensible and his eyes wandered to the writing which preceded them. It was a passage which had begun on the previous page and it started in mid-sentence.

... so the sheep preaches Love Thy Neighbour to the wolf and bleats The Meek Shall Inherit The Earth! And the tiger shall feed on grass; the shark devour seaweed; and the eagle eat the seeds of the sunflower!

The lust for blood will not be denied; it is integral to the human soul. Man's mind desires cruelty just as his body demands food – the doctrine of love springs from an infantile rejection of this truth and is a perverse denial of man's true nature.

Where it has had influence and has repressed man's

deep unconscious drives, religion has created effete societies beset by psychic disorders and neuroses. But in the main its adherents have paid only lip service to the concept of loving kindness – the most exquisite sufferings have been exacted in the name of God. Indeed, religion has been the very instrument of torture: Jews and Protestants died in thousands on Spanish bonfires; Dutch Catholics were racked in public until they begged to purchase their own execution – but termination of their pains was not for sale!

Today, theological pretexts have been replaced by political ones: Buchenwald, Nagasaki, Vietnam (and the world-wide use of torture by governments) show that sadism is not dead!

But the pursuit of cruelty *for its own sake* is imminent. Frank recognition of our basic appetites is spreading. A vigorous new cult of Nihilism and Satanism promises a renaissance of torture as an entertainment.

Dilke reread the passage with wide eyes, but his third reading was interrupted by a movement of the giant figure beside him. The curve of Lippe's mouth registered satisfaction as he crossed out the equation rewrote it in a revised form, punctuated it with an ex clamation mark and drew a line across the page beneath it. Then he leaned back and closed his eyes.

Dilke stared into the great features, so calm and benign in repose. Only the smoke moved in the stillness of the room. Spittle rattled in the bowl of Lippe's great pipe and he coughed softly, opened his eyes and began to write a fanciful reflection on the same theme as his previous entry.

Technology, Lippe wrote, could bring a new dimension to the pleasures of sadism. Advances in the technique of monitoring the activities of the brain permitted the recording of different kinds and degrees of suffering. A language of pain graphs would enable the sadist to recreate in his imagination the torments he had witnessed – just as the concert-goer relives his musical pleasures through a musical score!

And – Lippe continued – stimulation of the pain centres of a brain after its removal from the body would create pure pain; pain without physical manifestations; pain to be sensed intuitively, to be enjoyed on a mystical level.

Dilke's aversion to these bizarre notions of torture as an art-form and pain in a vacuum gave way to a new thought.

How serious were these jottings of Lippe's?

Was his previous hymn to a renaissance of sadism any less frivolous than the macabre fancies – triggered off by trifles read in a magazine – which now flowed from his pen?

The pen stopped writing. The writer gave a last glance at the image of the tortured rat before shutting the book and going to his bed; and Dilke crawled into his sleeping bag.

Dilke lay and blinked into the dark. Tired though he was his thoughts returned ceaselessly to Lippe's writings; were they the symptoms of paranoia or were they mere squibs, the products of a wickedly tasteless humour?

At last Dilke sank into a fitful sleep.

In the early hours of morning he had a strange dream in which he found himself, with the peculiar ambidexterity of the dreamer, occupying two different worlds simultaneously.

He floated in the depths of the sea. And he stood inside the head of Heinrich Lippe.

The cathedral of bone in which he stood was filled with dark and icy water. Dim shapes which thronged the water made swirling phosphorescent patterns all round him and the high vault echoed with shrieks of pain and laughter.

Dilke woke sweating and greeted the grey morning with a groan and a yawn, then he crawled from his refuge and scowled into the vast spaces of the dimly-lit room.

Dilke was extremely hungry. His stock of food was getting low, it was two days before Saturday's meeting and he had cut down on his eating.

Only two more days to Saturday! There would be four people plus Lippe and there was only one chair in Lippe's room. The meeting would almost certainly be in the conference room, but he would hang on here till the last moment to see and hear all he could. The conference room was on the same floor, only a few micro-miles along the corridor.

The cold light in the room grew warmer as dawn flushed the sky over the Andes and Dilke's spirits rose as he contemplated the approach of Saturday.

The first rays of sunlight shone through the windows and gilded the Peruvian urn on its pedestal.

'The professor is a great authority on the history of Peru.' Dilke remembered Cabral's nervous flattery and the relish with which he had explained the function of the vessel. On an impulse Dilke focused binoculars on the distant urn, then slowly tracked across the angular black, red and yellow design which covered the curved eathenware surface.

A formalized picture of Inca society was revealed. Men reaped corn, women washed clothes and children herded vicuna in the shadow of a huge, truncated pyramid of stone.

A writhing yellow sun was painted in the sky above it; and processions of figures mounted flights of steps cut in its steep sides: naked girls climbed one flight and priests carried the bound figures of young men up the other.

On the flattened top of the pyramid a priest with a towering head-dress held aloft the bleeding heart of a slain girl, while nearby, two priests thrust a trussed youth into a bath of flames. To the rigid formality of the painting the long dead artist had added startlingly violent and barbaric elements, a river of blood spouted from the sacrificial heart and tumbled down the steps, and the flames which twined like serpents around the burning body threw up lurid clouds of smoke. Yet the faces of victims and priests were equally without expression.

Dilke glimpsed framed pictures on the wall behind the urn and refocused his glasses to examine them in close up.

During Bellamy's brief tour of the paintings Cabral had enthusiastically estimated their value in escudos, and affirmed his boss's pre-eminence as a connoisseur of religious art.

Dilke swung his glasses from picture to picture. Innumerable saints, priests and crucifixions showed Lippe's interest in Christianity, and his preoccupation with its more sombre aspects.

Saints endured the last transports of martyrdom.

Goya's clergy flew like vampires through the air, and screams split the faces of Bacon's blood-spattered cardinals. Kneelers at the foot of a cross were shown, by the power of Dilke's binoculars, to be less than devout: the anguish of Christ brought no tears of pity to the eyes of the multitude which the Flemish painter had clothed in the costume of his time and place and invested with every sort of ugliness and depravity. Their palms were pressed together but their features gleamed with a sly and tainted pleasure.

Lippe had found a painter who shared his views! Dilke lowered his glasses, and prepared for another day in the old man's grim company.

14

After a closed-circuit check on factory and labs, Lippe's morning and afternoon activities went on as usual, but in the evening he changed the pattern of his day by switching on the television for a second time.

Both screens lit up; at first they were so dim that Dilke could see nothing but two spots of light in the top screen. Through the speaker he heard a gruff voice, a laugh, the strident evensong of cicadas. Now he saw that the two lights were white and perfect circles; beneath a full moon its reflected twin swayed gently on dark water.

Lippe reached out and touched a switch and both screens were flooded with brilliant light.

The lower picture was photographed from below water; the dark shapes of fish drifted between the camera and an underwater spotlight.

The upper picture showed an expanse of water in the foreground, lapping gently against the curve of Lippe's terrace wall. At the end of the wall Dilke saw and recognized the towering metal structure beneath which he had once walked.

Something moved on the platform.

A mule which stood at the top of the chute, with two swarthy men close behind, flicked its long ears nervously and snorted anxiously at the water below. A man clapped it on the flank; the mule reared back in alarm and crashed into a gate which had been shut behind it. The second man drained a can of beer and dropped it over the rail, then grabbed the beast's tail and twisted it viciously up and over its rump.

Lippe leaned forward and turned up the sound.

Dilke felt a dreadful foreboding.

The mule stumbled. The man jabbed a stick up under its tail, its hooves slipped on to the chute and it rattled down the steep incline to a chorus of hoots, sitting back absurdly on its hindquarters with its forelegs straight and stiff. At the bottom it gave an awkward leap and hit the lake in a cloud of spray.

An explosion of foam suddenly appeared in the lower screen as the heavy body and flailing hooves churned the water.

In the upper screen the beast's head rose from the surface of the lake and as its panic decreased it swam ponderously in a wide arc towards the shore.

It was almost out of camera range when a long rope which tied it to the platform jerked it to a stop; the rope snapped out of the water in a shower of sparkling drops; the once sluggish fish streaked across the lower screen towards the floundering beast.

An agonized scream burst from the mule's jaws with such horrifying power that the sound buzzed and crackled in the speaker and Dilke's hair stood out stiff on his scalp.

The stretched head and neck vanished from the upper screen and appeared in the lower one spouting fountains of bubbles from its gaping mouth and nostrils.

Piranhas flew in hundreds through a storm of blood; ripping, chopping, tearing at the hulk of flesh; dismembering the great body.

The dying beast sank. Its frantic struggles weakened as it was stripped of muscle and sinew; ropes of gut entangled its kicking legs; a leg and shoulder swung loose from the rib-cage; bones gleamed faintly, then disappeared into the depths of the lake.

A fish nosed ravenously through swirling blood then swooped after its vanished prey.

A sound of heavy breathing filled the room.

The underwater struggle had been uncannily silent; only the slap of water on the shore of the lake had accompanied the violence beneath its surface.

Dilke came out of a trance of horror to hear the first, cautious return of a cicada's song; and Lippe's hoarse breathing.

Lippe stared at the empty screen with a corner of his mouth hitched up in a loose smile. Points of reflected light from the television glowed on the glassy surface of his great eyes like blue flames seen through furnace doors.

Mathew Dilke shuddered. Behind the blotched and wrinkled facade of age burned an ageless, boundless, infinitely evil power.

Heinrich Lippe radiated evil.

Dilke looked with loathing at the immense figure which lay back in the shadows of the chair staring fixedly at the dancing network of light in the floodlit water.

The urgent rhythm of Lippe's breathing had not diminished after the mule disappeared. Now the wheezing was more laboured and the crooked smile faded from his lips. He coughed to free the constriction in his chest. The first cough detonated others, until his body shook and the chair bucked madly, throwing Dilke flat on his face.

Lippe swung round to the desk, pressed down on his knees with clenched fists – a burnt-out pipe clutched in one of them – and abandoned himself to a paroxysm of coughing. In the light of the desk-lamp his face was puffed and mottled with purple and his swollen jowls were flushed with blood.

'Cough your guts up.'

Dilke's voice was cold and flat as Lippe hooked out a waste-bin from under the desk and spat copiously into it.

The phlegm was colourless. It was followed by more phlegm, dredged up from the bottom of the great lungs, as yellow as chicken-fat and streaked with red. For a long time Lippe leaned over the arm of the chair then he slumped back, wiped his sweating face and stared bleakly into the dark with a handkerchief to his lips.

Dilke's hatred of Lippe was reborn. Now it burned like a fire of ice at the centre of his being.

When Lippe left, Dilke crawled from his narrow den and stood up. Moonlight made a shining path along the ridge of the great curved chairback and Dilke stalked along it with his head down and hands thrust deep into jacket pockets.

Lippe was no mere fantasist.

His sadism was not confined to words.

Visions of the night's appalling entertainment would not be erased from Dilke's mind. In his memory the stricken beast kicked and bled.

He walked half-way round the curve of the chairback, to the point where he had climbed up the zip-fastener, and looked out towards the terrace and lake. The gaunt shape of the plastic-coated horse stood like a ghost in the moonlight.

The horse which was a mule! A giant amongst mules. A player from Lippe's private theatre of cruelty (dragged from the water before its final dissolution) and a monument to Lippe's depravity.

Dilke shivered and turned away.

Only faint rectangles of reflected light from the framed pictures relieved the darkness in the room. A smell of stale tobacco-smoke and, Dilke fancied, a sickly-sweet breath of corruption floated up from the vast space between the arms of the chair. Suddenly the darkness seemed to be thick with a brooding, malevolent presence; a presence which filled the room and spread into the rest of the building and beyond. Dilke felt the prick of sweat on his forehead then he hunched his shoulders and hurried back to his sanctuary on the southern wing of the chair.

Dilke peered at his watch and closed his eyes again. It was still early.

Some lesser mysteries were now explained: now he knew the purpose of the lakeside platform; the origin of the rusting cans beneath it; the reason for the shouts and splashings he had heard when lying in the insect's egg nine days ago.

Discovery of the grim reason for the traffic in mules had destroyed Whitehall's theory that they were germ-lab animals. The big mystery of Lippe's preoccupation with psychobiological experiments remained unsolved; but Dilke still had faith that his presence at

Lippe's Saturday meeting with Bodovsky and the rest would give him the key to that mystery.

He moved restlessly in his sleeping bag and wished the hours away.

Lippe arrived before nine and brusquely summoned his assistant, then fidgeted round the room until the German arrived carrying plans for a factory extension.

'No, Schmidt!' the old man waved aside the drawings. 'Leave everything and work up here today. And Schmidt,' the German paused at the laboratory door, 'you have thirty hours.'

The old man spent most of the day in the laboratory with Schmidt, returning occasionally to answer his phone or to stand at the window and gaze at the distant mountains.

Dilke kept watch on his comings and goings until late afternoon when, as he was about to leave on his journey to the conference room, both men came out of the laboratory.

The professor seated himself before the television as his assistant switched it on; then Schmidt stood back, laid a hand on the wing of the chair and took a notepad from his pocket.

The weight of the hand on the chair squeezed air along the leather pipeline; stale air which had stagnated inside the piping ever since the chair had been made, and which now rushed past Dilke and out through the gap his grenade had made. He lay on his belly and stared at the screen.

A picture appeared and Dilke recognized, with a start, the room in which Bellamy had slept.

There was no one in sight, but a heap of clothes on the floor and the hiss of water from the bathroom showed that the suite was occupied.

The sound of the shower stopped and a naked man walked into the picture. He dried himself sketchily and discarded the wet towel, then he lit a cigar, poured himself a drink and lay back on the bed.

'This is Julius Botticelli, Herr Professor,' Schmidt said.

Botticelli was a heavyweight gone to fat; thin on top but with an excessively hairy torso and hair sprouting from each shoulder.

Schmidt looked down at his notes. 'Julius Botticelli directs Antimob, an American law-enforcement organization which is employed by many city authorities to supplement their undermanned police forces. Before the growth of student unrest and black militancy Antimob was a security firm called American Property Protection Incorporated. Since Julius Botticelli joined the company, and it changed from conventional property-protection to freelance riot-control, it has grown into what is virtually a small private army, with its own helicopters, armoured vehicles and heavy-calibre automatic weapons. Botticelli is on the far political Right. The unions hate him because he has been involved in strike-breaking. And the radicals accuse him of instigating riots by using agents provocateurs.'

Schmidt paused and Lippe sucked on his pipe.

'Is there anything else, Schmidt?'

'Yes, Herr Professor. Before he joined Antimob he was in the National Guard, where he wrote a training manual on riot control.' Schmidt glanced at the old man, 'He is a strong advocate of the use of gas.'

On the screen before them the naked man lay on his back on the bed, wreathed in cigar smoke, slowly turning the pages of a book. It was not a book about riot control;

Dilke recognized the imprint of lipsticked lips on the cover. Botticelli turned the book sideways to get a different angle on sexy Samantha, then reached for his drink.

There was a click of glass on glass as he replaced the tumbler on the bedside cabinet, and Dilke suddenly realized how clearly even the smallest sound came over the television speaker.

The click of a glass. The turn of a page. The creak of a bed.

Dilke's heart gave a great leap and sweat broke out on his face and body.

Before they had gone into Lima with Cabral he had talked to Gilbert Bellamy in that room! With a thudding heart Dilke remembered Bellamy talking while knotting his tie at the wardrobe mirror, and *he* had replied over the Aid's speaker from a jacket hanging on a chairback.

Dilke cursed bitterly. Lippe must have watched and listened! Bellamy's quiet exchanges with a disembodied voice must have perplexed him, but would have been enough to arouse his suspicion – and lead to Bellamy's death.

Air rushed back into the pipeline as Schmidt lifted his great hand from the chair to switch to another channel; and Dilke wiped his sweating forehead with a sleeve and stared at the new picture.

It showed Cabral's hospitality lounge, its technicoloured exuberance translated into sober black and white. Two men sat side by side on the sofa while Cabral tinkered with bottles and glasses at his cocktail cabinet and talked plastics across the room.

The Portuguese brought drinks to the low table, raised his glass to Soviet/Peruvian amity then started his spiel again. The Russians nursed their vodkas and gave him their stolid attention.

Schmidt silenced Cabral with a twist of the volume control, leaving him to mouth silently at his guests, and cleared his throat. 'The man on the right, Herr Professor, is Colonel Eugene Bodovsky of the Russian Military Intelligence Corps. He visited you during October last year, but made no decision about making a purchase.'

Lippe waved a hand impatiently, 'I remember, Schmidt.'

'His companion on this visit is Colonel Makhov.'

Bodovsky and Makhov were out of the same mould; they had the same square builds, flat Slav faces, cropped heads. Both wore dark suits of a conservative cut; Makhov, the younger man by twenty years, wore spectacles without rims.

'Colonel Makhov is an expert in weaponry, Herr Professor.'

There was a long silence, broken at last by the old man.

'Is that all, Schmidt?'

'He is a *technician*, Professor.'

Lippe looked reflectively at the screen. 'Then they must be interested,' he murmured. 'Yes, Schmidt, this time they will buy. Now! Tell me about Kirangozi.'

'I regret that I cannot show you President Kirangozi, Herr Professor. Since he flew in from Liberia on Wednesday he has been staying in Lima and he has postponed his arrival here until tomorrow.'

'The information I have concerning the president is that his presidency is threatened by political rivals who have provoked tribes in the Liberian interior to rebel against the government. The army is loyal to him, but the country's interior favours guerilla fighters, and the

rebels are receiving weapons from neighbouring countries.'

Schmidt had no more information. He switched off
Cabral's dumb mouthings and returned to the laboratory
with his master, and Dilke lay and brooded at the
entrance of his tunnel.

What had Bodovsky not purchased last October? *What*
were they interested in now, and would buy this time?

But Dilke's mind was not wholly on the Russians.
Fragmentary thoughts and feelings about other things
filled his head. Half-formed thoughts which over-
shadowed the question of the Russian presence in Peru.

Dilke stared at the blank screen and saw Gilbert
Bellamy again, tying his tie and talking to an empty
room. Dilke's belief that they had been overheard grew
more certain – and he bitterly recalled that he had
spoken the first words.

But there *may* have been *other* betrayals. Lippe may
also have watched Bellamy when he looked at the folders
in Schmidt's small laboratory.

Dilke sourly recognized the thought as an attempt to
diminish remorse. He ate the last of his rations (he had
saved enough for a big meal), strapped on his crossbow
and grenade harness and struck camp.

Dilke's descent of the chair was a lot faster than his climb
up it, for he had no food to carry, and before he set off
he tossed his bedroll into space and watched it fall, until
it lay, a barely visible speck of blue on the dark floor,
one thousand five hundred micro-feet below.

Three hours later he reached the floor, then he crossed
the room and walked under the door into the corridor
which led to the conference chamber.

Half-way along the passageway a closed door marked

the limits of Professor Lippe's personal territory. Beyond it the austere black floor-covering changed to a thick green carpet: a wall-to-wall forest of twisted nylon strands. Dilke avoided it by climbing on to a skirting board. He had almost reached the entrance to the conference room along this wide highway when the door behind him opened and Schmidt came through it carrying a tray. The German passed him with earthshaking strides; Dilke had a flashing vision of vast, frayed trouser turn-ups and heard a rattle of jars on the huge tray; then the German went into the conference room, soon to reappear without the tray and march off down the corridor towards the lift.

Schmidt had put out the corridor lights. It was too dark to descend from the skirting board and it would be impossible to find a way into the room before morning. Dilke lay down and listened to the whisper of carpet fibres slowly rising as they recovered from the crushing weight of the German's feet.

15

When it was barely light Dilke cautiously descended a hundred micro-feet to the floor, fumbling for hand and footholds in the fissure between skirting board and door-frame. He passed under the door, then climbed on to the skirting board which ran along the southern wall of the conference room. Across the dark floor, almost a micro-mile away, the table loomed up like a flat-topped mountain. He travelled along the skirting until he was opposite the long, southern side of the table. His position, so near the floor and so far away from the table, was not ideal for eavesdropping; he would be unable to see and, perhaps, to hear anyone seated to the north of it.

In the growing light, the dark carpet had become a deep shade of green and he could see some detail in the structure of the table. Attached to its underside was the box into which he had been dropped by Lippe on the night of his capture; in the front of the box was the hole into which the old man had put his hand to mix his gaseous brew. And, above the circular entrance to the glove there were two hardly discernible notches in the edge of the table top.

Dilke got out his binoculars. Now he could see the edge of the hinged glass lid to the recessed box; at each side of the glass was a narrow gap where it fitted flush with the table-top. Tiny gaps, only a millimetre wide, but enough for him to squeeze into if he could climb up there.

He lowered his field-glasses.

In the shadows beneath the table he saw a thick column joining box to floor: a duct for drawing away gas – he remembered the yellow vapour disappearing from the box after the death of the army of ants.

Without hesitation he climbed down to the carpet and headed for the duct.

The nylon strands were twice his height and set close together. He toiled on between them, crawling under and over smooth ropes which curled and twined around the main hauser-like fibres. The duct was not visible from the depths of this man-made jungle but he was able to judge direction from occasional glimpses of the table.

His jacket was stained black with sweat when he came at last to the base of the duct. It was made of steel plates welded together at the edges, and formed a great column six inches square and two feet high, which was joined to the side of the box. He laid back his head and stared up. The box was also of steel construction; its bottom fractionally overlapped its side walls, making a narrow ledge all round its base. A ledge which would serve as a footpath when he reached it; for he was confident that he could climb the duct – the welding at its corners was as rough to a man of his stature as a rock-face.

The difficult stretch might be the last third of the climb: from the ledge up on to the top of the table.

He would worry about that when he got there.

He tightened his grenade belt, secured his crossbow

harness and started to climb.

By midday he had reached the ledge. He walked along it and rounded the south-eastern corner on to the ledge along the front of the box. The sunlight dazzled him after the darkness under the table. He squinted down at the carpet, which looked deceptively smooth from six hundred micro-feet up, then turned to the three-hundred micro-foot wall which he still had to climb. The metal was faced with veneered plywood; Dilke anxiously searched for a way up its polished surface. A panel of three switches was recessed into the wood immediately above him. Above *them* was the enormous, round entrance to the cavernous glove. He could climb up the edge of the switch panel as far as the glove, but then get no higher.

He hurried back to the corner of the box (hoping that the end of the three-ply sheet would be climbable) to find that adhesive had oozed out between wood and metal; and he discovered, to his delight, that a fuzz of fine threads and particles of dust had stuck to it before it dried.

The line of the join led straight to one of the gaps in the edge of the table. Dilke jumped, grabbed a hanging thread, and scrambled upwards.

The space between the glass lid and the adjacent wooden surface made a narrow trench right across the top of the table. He crawled into it after an arduous half-hour's climb. His hands were stiff and sore and his whole body ached after being on the move for eight hours without a break.

Though he was bone-weary he was elated, for the trench gave him perfect concealment and a panoramic view of the room.

He stood with his head and shoulders above table level and gazed around. The door was to the south, wide windows were to the west, and a glass-fronted display case of plastic-ware covered most of the northern wall. But the thing which held Dilke's eyes was on the table before him. The tray which Schmidt had left in the room the previous night was only a yard away, and on it were five jars full of yellow crystals. Each jar was labelled, and written on each label was a single word followed by a roman numeral: FRAT I, FRAT II, FRAT III, FRAT IV, FRAT V.

Dilke's eyes blazed with excitement.

Already, even before the meeting had begun (he glanced at his watch – *still* an hour to go) he had made a discovery.

Within those towering jars lay the reason for Lippe's meeting. FRAT was a chemical, not a biological organism!

Dilke stared at the crystals until points of sunlight shining from their faceted surfaces danced before his eyes. He checked the time again, then climbed out of his slit trench, walked on to the glass and looked down into the box. The red glove was just discernible through the reflected image of the room ceiling; he lay face down on the cold surface, shaded his eyes with his hands and peered down.

Now he could see the glove clearly, also the two beakers he had seen on the night he had been precipitated into the box. The wall which had separated him from the army ants had been removed, and today there were no ants.

Instead, there were four creatures which Dilke did not see at first because they were so still. In each shadowy corner squatted a huge scorpion. Each one was fully eight inches long, armed with half-inch stings at the ends of segmented tails. Though he was safe from them he gave an involuntary shiver, then he watched them with fascination, wishing to see them move.

Schmidt entered the room with a pile of note-pads and a handful of ballpoint pens and Dilke slid back into the trench. The German furnished the table meticulously with six pads and six biros, switched on a coffee percolator on a side table, set out half a dozen cups beside it, then returned to the main table and looked down at it with his hands thrust into the pockets of a freshly-starched white coat. He stood for a long time; his bony face without expression; his single eye fixed unwinkingly on the tray of jars.

Dilke watched him narrowly from the trench. The man had a gaunt and sombre power; what power did the old man possess to dominate so formidable a servant?

The door opened and the professor came in. Schmidt gave a start and turned towards him. The old man's faded blue shirt and slacks were clean and pressed, his hair was brushed and his face wore a hint of the good humour he reserved for customers. He crossed the room, bent over the table to examine the scorpions and rattle his fingernails on the glass, then looked around with satisfaction at the preparations for the meeting.

At two-thirty voices outside preceded the arrival of Cabral and his party; the sales manager ushered in Botticelli and the Russians, explained to the professor in an undertone that Kirangozi would be a few minutes late, then hurried off to meet the African's car.

Professor Lippe offered cigars, Schmidt poured coffee and they all sat down at the long table.

They had finished coffee when Kirangozi made his entrance. The Liberian president was hugely obese; a beaming Negro who spoke Oxford English; had welted tribal scars on his fat black cheeks; wore a dark pinstripe suit, lilac shirt, lavender silk tie and an explosive purple handkerchief in his breast pocket.

Six pairs of staring eyes followed him to his seat.

The old man greeted him, then leaned his elbows on the table, turned slowly from guest to guest, and addressed them in a voice scarcely higher than his normal hoarse whisper:

'Now that we are gathered together, gentlemen, I am happy to welcome you all to Peru,' Lippe's manner was cordial but a light touch of emphasis on *now* expressed disapproval of late-coming, 'and I am confident that the outcome of this meeting will be to our mutual benefit. We are all aware that this meeting is of a confidential nature and for my part I promise that it will remain so.

'The door, if you please, Schmidt.'

Schmidt, who had been waiting near the door, opened it momentarily, revealing a uniformed guard in the corridor, then closed it and underlined Lippe's promise with the click of a key in the lock.

Four pairs of expressionless eyes – the Liberian's smile had faded – returned to the old man's face.

'You will forgive me, gentlemen, if I do not come directly to the subject of my talk. You may think it a digression, but first I wish to describe to you an experience I had when occupied on research in Berlin during the autumn of the year 1944.

'A colleague of mine at the Academy of Science, a neurologist, was engaged in research into methods of ideological re-education, or thought reform. To this end he was conducting animal experiments to discover the sources of the intellect and the emotions. In his experiments (which are a commonplace today), he was searching for links between psychological and physiological states ...'

167

Lippe's audience displayed little curiosity about the activities of his neurologist friend.

'. . . and one day I happened, by chance, to witness one of these experiments. As I entered his laboratory he introduced a mouse into the cage of a cat. The cat, which was large and hungry, crouched, ready to spring. Then its demeanour changed dramatically: instead of pouncing on the mouse, it rushed away in extreme terror and crouched in the corner, leaping frantically into the air every time the mouse ran near to it.

'And the reason for this extraordinary volte-face? A small charge of electrical energy, conveyed to the brain along a wire implanted in the brain tissue!

'I cannot express to you the excitement I felt on witnessing this total reversal of the animal's natural instincts and, being a chemist, I wondered if the same effect could be triggered-off by chemical means.

'I conducted experiments of my own, injecting solutions into different parts of the brain, and successfully induced in various animals such emotions as excitement, rage, affection, agitation and sexual passion. I had begun attempts to induce these reactions by means of inhalation instead of injection, when, unfortunately, the fall of the Reich ended my work for many years.

'Years later, here in Peru, I recommenced my experiments,' Lippe smiled, 'and, now, gentlemen, you may observe their results.'

He nodded curtly at his assistant: there was a swish of venetian blinds and the room went dark, the click of a switch and the recessed box in the table lit up.

Dilke's view was more restricted than before; he could see only two scorpions, but he could see them very clearly under the bright lights.

Both scorpions were female, and the back of each one

was covered with miniature replicas of herself; their tiny legs, claws and tails were interlocked, making a living cloak on each mother's body. The broods shifted restlessly under the sudden glare and heat of the light, and one mother raised a huge claw and gently pushed back infants which wandered on to her head.

Dilke heard Lippe's voice in the darkness.

'The scorpion is a maligned creature, gentlemen. Her savagery is much exaggerated. For weeks these females have lived together in perfect amity, and you see with what solicitude they treat their children. We must see what we can do about that! Yes, Schmidt.'

The red glove under the glass trembled and stiffened as the German's hand entered it and poured the liquid from one beaker on to the crystals in the other. Before the fumes which erupted from the crystals had thinned to a pale mist four scorpions met in the middle of the box with a crash; Dilke felt the shock beneath his feet. The four families were shaken loose from their mothers' backs and hit the box lid with a rattle like stones thrown at a window. To a staccato accompaniment of crashes and cracks the scorpions fought, hurtling from side to side of the box, while their children fought small-scale wars of their own. Dilke heard legs being snapped and claws being crushed and twisted from their sockets. Within minutes only one adult survived; scrabbling about on three legs, crushing infants with nutcracker claws, while others clung to her and stabbed her plated body with baby stings.

The Negro snickered in the dark. Across the table his three fellow spectators crouched and stared down into the arena. Lippe's elbow rested on the table only inches away from Dilke's trench. Beyond and above the ridge of the massive forearm Dilke saw the professor's great head turn slowly as he sardonically watched the rapt faces of his guests. Then the old man reached down and switched off the light in the box and the blind which covered the picture window was raised by his assistant.

The show was over.

The four watchers sat back blinking. Lit from below their faces had seemed demonic, but in the harsh light of day their expressions were merely vicious.

The bloody conflict they had seen was a theatrical high spot in a carefully rehearsed programme, but as drama it seemed incomplete. They fixed their eyes on the old man and eagerly waited for him to speak.

The professor took his time. He had produced a pipe and had struck a match and his words were punctuated with blurts of smoke from his thin lips.

'You have just witnessed a reversal of the most powerful of social instincts. You have seen the affection which is shared by parents and offspring, extinguished with a whiff of gas!'

With a flick of the wrist Lippe extinguished the burning match and dropped it into his coffee cup, then he removed the pipe stem from his mouth.

A chill seized Dilke's back and his heart pounded against his ribs. Now was the moment! The words Lippe had just spoken *must* be the preface to final disclosure!

Lippe began to speak. 'I have created a unique weapon. It is the gas I have just demonstrated. It is as effective against humans as against invertebrates. When inhaled it induces a murderous frenzy which the victim directs at members of his own species. Use it against your enemies and it will trigger off their mutual destruction: worker will kill brother worker, and soldier will kill brother soldier. I call it *Fratricide*!'

As Lippe paused to relish his *mot juste* Dilke's

thoughts ran wildly on ... and man will kill wife, wife kill son, son kill sister ...

'What economy of effort, gentlemen. The enemy destroys himself.' Lippe smiled. 'Do you not agree that this is the most elegant of all possible weapons?'

The gentlemen did not return his smile, but a glance between the Russians disclosed a guarded satisfaction, and the eyes of the Negro and the American glittered with anticipation of future battles won.

16

Rage shook the pit of Dilke's stomach. One thing was sure! Lippe was not in this for mere profit, he was not just a merchant of death. Lippe was an apostle of extermination, an agent of apocalypse, a sadist on a global scale. And *Fratricide* was the loathsome flower of his corrupt and teeming creative genius.

A lust to kill Lippe swept through Dilke; followed by bitter disgust at his powerlessness to do so.

A fusillade of cracks, like muffled pistol shots, broke the silence of the room as another dozen infants were swept up and crushed in the scorpion's claws.

Dilke crouched in the trench and glared up at Heinrich Lippe. Crossbow and grenades were *nothing* against this human monster. But there *was* a weapon (the snarl of frustration fell from Dilke's face), the most elegant of all possible weapons! It lay behind him, it measured one foot by three feet by four feet, it was boxed in steel and glass and was ready for use. Its name was *Fratricide*.

Dilke spun round and stared at the side of the trench. The edge of the plate-glass lid was about five to six microfeet deep; it was pulled down tight by the low atmos-

pheric pressure within the box and bedded firmly on a
rubber seal. It was sea-green and as smooth and thick as
polar ice.

Too bloody thick to blast with grenades.

Dilke stared down furiously into the reservoir of gas.
Through the shining reflective surface he could see the
battle of extinction still raging (and feel its vibration
beneath his feet) and the red rubber hand protruding
into the box ...

The professor had reached the end of his pregnant
pause; he pushed aside the coffee cup and drew the tray
of jars towards him.

And the red rubber glove protruded into the box!

Dilke dived for the open end of the trench and
scrambled down towards the ledge far below; the ledge
which led to the entrance to the glove. He descended
recklessly, halving the time it had taken to climb up.
Above the sound of his own heavy breathing he could
hear the old man eloquently listing the virtues of the
gas: silent, invisible, lethal; cheap to produce; long shelf-
life; easy dissemination (from air, sea, land; by grenade,
bomb, shell, spray, missile); harmless to property (leaving enemy plant intact); pin-point accuracy not needed.
'A man is a small target for a gun,' Lippe murmured,
'but his *lungs* have an area of two hundred square metres.
With *gas*, the target is as big as a tennis court! And a
tree or a trench won't shelter him from it ...'

Dilke paused for breath at the entrance to the glove. The
inside was a vast rounded cave. In the distance were
entrances to five lesser caves: a row of four and, to their
left and sloping downwards, a wider tunnel for a thumb.
The heavy smell of sweating rubber, and lingering smells
from Schmidt's hand of chemicals and mouse ordure,

filled the air. Dilke hurried into the glove's interior and ran into the first of the four tunnels. At the end of the tunnel he unslung his bow and carefully fired nine percussion bolts (all that he had) into the wall, spacing the holes evenly round the circumference of its curved surface.

This would take more than one grenade: he unzipped all the pouches, emptied them on to the floor and went down on his knees; he breathed deeply, quickly pulled the pin out of each grenade then jumped up and raced out of the tunnel; he turned right at its exit, flung himself down the slope of the tunnel next to it and rolled into its rounded end.

The grenades went off with a deep thudding shock like a harpoon exploding inside a whale. The glove juddered with the impact. Dilke staggered out of his shelter and stood on the shaking floor of the outer cavern. Light shone through the hole in the tip of the index finger and wind whistled through it, equalizing the air pressure between room and box. Dilke could hear nothing – the blast had deafened him – but he felt the wind on his back. Then, as the air pressure stabilized, the wind dropped and changed direction and he felt the flow of gas on his face as it drifted through the glove and out into the conference room. The gas was invisible – its colour had leached away – but it pricked his eyes and smarted in his nostrils. He went inside the finger and looked out through the breach in its tip and felt the gas, warmed by the lights which had illuminated the box, on his skin.

There was a sudden crack in Dilke's eardrums and his hearing came back. He heard the scuffle of scorpions and the distant sound of Lippe's voice echoing through the cavernous glove. The grenades must have been like the outbreak of scorpion warfare all over again; but **Lippe's** voice went imperturbably on.

Dilke stared through the ragged hole in the rubber, then turned and moved back into the glove with the deliberation of a sleep-walker. Waves of red and purple and black moved before him. The sound of blood in his ears was like the beat of the sea. The interior of the blood-red glove seemed to pulse to its rhythm as if he was passing through the chambers of a great heart. He stood at the circular entrance of the glove, and he heard Lippe's voice, but the words were without meaning, like the sound of a dead language, or the deep sonorities of massed choirs.

Dilke was almost unaware of his long climb back to the surface of the table-top.

He crawled into the trench, then climbed out of it on to the glass and stood, oblivious of the chance of being seen, and stared at the figures around the table.

Dilke's whole being was filled with one emotion; a deep, dark, bottomless malevolence which excluded all other feeings.

It was without the passionate and personal quality of his previous hatred of Lippe, for no memory of **Lippe's** person and actions remained in Dilke's mind.

He looked with impartial and brooding intensity at the mountains of flesh which surrounded him, then he watched the movements of Lippe's great mouth and stared at the jar which Lippe held in his giant hand.

Fratricide one, Lippe explained, was a blockbuster: the first gas he had created and still the most potent. Two, three and four had varying degrees of volatility to give flexibility to the range. The fifth gas was in a different category.

'It is the newest member of the family, gentlemen.'

He rotated the jar of crystals, spinning reflected points of sunlight on to the ceiling and into the narrowed eyes of his listeners.

'Frat. five is a political weapon, not a military weapon. It is not the original gas in diluted form but has a different formula. It inflames passions, but does not instigate mass homicide. It is a manipulative agent, a chemical agent provocateur, a strategic weapon for the forces of law ...'

Lippe's voice became louder and hoarser. 'Introduced into a campus or a ghetto, this gas will create an explosion of violent behaviour, and as the start of the rioting can be predetermined, adequate forces for its repression can be assembled in advance.'

The gas in the glass-topped box slowly filtered through the glove and into the room. It floated up and mingled with the pipe and cigar smoke which overhung the long table and it infiltrated the nostrils, the lungs, the blood and the central nervous systems of the seated men.

A violent tremor shook Lippe's hand and the yellow crystals rattled in the jar.

The air was heavy with repressed violence.

Kirangozi wiped his sweating face and scowled across the table at the American. Botticelli savagely rolled a cigar butt in his enormous jaws. Schmidt's great thumb click-click, click-clicked the plunger of a ball-point pen. Makhov turned and glared at Bodovsky as his companion swung a crossed leg and his knee thudded against the underside of the table.

Lippe began again.

Now he spoke a jumble of disconnected sentences, like bits from a torn-up speech. Isolated sentences were lucid; put together they made nonsense. He spoke harshly with shuddering pauses for breath, and his face darkened as he worked himself into a shrill and passionate rage.

Dilke crouched at the edge of the table and felt each jarring blow of the Russian's knee beneath it, and he stared into the old man's snarling face and shared his mindless fury.

Lippe jumped up and hurled down the jar. Glass splinters and shattered crystals flew into the air. Lippe stamped and jumped and flailed hysterically at the table with his flat hands. A torrent of German obscenities and the rattle of loose dentures flew from his mouth in a shower of spittle and Schmidt rose and took his master by the back of his neck and smashed his head on the table top.

17

A bomb of rage exploded in the locked room. Its shock-waves rocked the table. With a crash of overturned chairs, Lippe's guests scrambled up and lunged murderously at each other. A black storm of rage and hate, of blood and pain and death filled the air. Towering mountains of bone and muscle collided furiously. The vast plateau of the table-top quaked and shook. Dilke danced joyfully across its shining surface and capered and howled at the centre of the holocaust.

Lippe's great skull rang dully the first time it hit the solid teak and Schmidt smashed it down again with maniacal violence as it rebounded. At the second impact the skull cracked. Dilke shouted exultantly at the third, fourth and fifth soggy blows then the German released his hold and his master slid off the table and disappeared under it.

Biting and butting and gouging, the men fought with a primeval lack of skill and a bestial disregard for their own injuries; they lurched and brawled amongst broken chairs; sometimes in a single bellowing scrum, sometimes in changing, indiscriminate groups of two or three.

The guard in the corridor leaned on the broad window-ledge with a cigarette poised half way to his lips; then he turned away from the sunlit vista of hills and valleys and stared at the door of the conference room.

For an hour the professor's low voice had been almost inaudible in the corridor, and its rising volume and increasing stridency had been muffled by the heavy door; but now the guard could hear a series of thuds and crashes and the sound of raised voices. He tossed the cigarette through the open window with a backward swing of his arm, and frowned uncertainly at the closed door.

The noises grew louder. The guard stepped forward, removed his peaked cap and, as he pressed an ear against the door, his eyes flew open wide and sweat broke out on his forehead. The sound was like a cage full of fighting baboons.

He looked anxiously up and down the corridor, then slipped his revolver from its holster and turned the door handle.

The door was locked. Something inside crashed against it and the guard jumped back. He took a small step towards the lift, then, with sudden decision, he snatched his automatic rifle from the window sill, and swung it butt first against the lock, and the door flew open.

The clothes of the five men were ripped and their faces and bodies ran with blood.

The Russian colonels screamed a furious, wordless, primal language unknown to modern man. Makhov had pinned his comrade against a wall and was hammering his face with both fists.

The Liberian president lay on his back near the door with the knee of the boss of Antimob stuck into his great paunch and his swollen puce tongue ballooning from his mouth. Kirangozi was dead, but Botticelli's thick fingers were still buried in the Negro's fat black neck and a guttural sound, like the growl of a great beast over a fresh kill, rattled deep in the American's throat. Schmidt stood over them with a broken chair raised high above his head.

The guard saw it all in a flash as the door burst open, and he ducked as Schmidt threw the chair at him. The German had lost his glasses; the guard saw an empty and inflamed eye socket next to the single glaring eye and he pulled the trigger as Schmidt leapt at him across the sprawling figures.

The burst of rifle bullets knocked Schmidt back; the guard coughed and grunted as he got a lungful of gas; then he sprayed the room with automatic fire and Dilke heard splintering wood, breaking glass and the thud of bullets hitting flesh.

The guard rushed from the room; Dilke heard his pounding feet and the clash of lift gates.

A current of air flowed between the broken conference room windows and the window in the corridor; wind swept the table top, rolling the acrid gunsmoke before it and sweeping away the gas. Dilke's corrosive rage went with it.

The wind fluttered the pages of the notepads and drove a great cylinder of cigar-ash across the surface of the table.

Dilke heard distant shouts and screams, the faint stutter of the gun, and the sound of more glass breaking.

The wind got behind the door and slammed it shut. Then there was silence.

The pages were still. The grey cylinder of ash, which had trundled across the table into the smear of blood, was still.

The rigid muscles of Dilke's belly and limbs went slack, he dropped limply to his knees, rolled back on to the cold glass and stared at the ceiling. After an eternity of silence he turned over. Genocide had run its course: he saw below him the remains of the four scorpion families scattered over the floor of the box.

He rose and looked about. From the centre of the table, the floor and the bodies upon it were not visible. The room which had been so full of conflict now seemed empty and at peace.

Dilke swayed and stepped forward dizzily towards the trench and the way to the floor.

He saw the bodies on his way down.

The three near the door were sprawled in violently twisted attitudes, but Lippe lay on his side beneath the table as if he were asleep, with his head propped against the steel duct, his knees slightly bent, his ankles neatly together and his arms extended before him.

Dilke was hardly conscious of his descent. He climbed automatically, dazed by the silence and dazzled by the sunlight which illuminated the frozen chaos of the room. He reached the carpet and looked up into Lippe's great face. Seen from below and at close range – he was only a foot away – the illusion that Lippe slept was banished.

The massive head-wound was not in sight (only a drop of dry blood, which had run down the cheek and hung suspended under the curve of the chin, showed that the wound existed) but the angle of head to body was grot-

esquely unnatural and the bones of the head were fractured and displaced. Beneath the skin the facial structure
had slipped and Lippe's features were curiously askew.
The mouth hung open revealing a bottom row of teeth;
the upper plate had fallen on to the carpet and the face
expressed a sort of dolorous surprise at its presence
there; the hooded eyelids were lifted high and the pupils
had swung down (as if by their own dark weight) to stare
at the vagrant teeth.

Lippe was dead, but a sluggish rearguard action
against the inevitable corruption of his flesh went on; his
hair and nails still grew and hormone and enzyme fac-
tories deep inside him had not quite shut down.

Dilke heard sounds like distant thunder and looked
with wonder at the receding contours of the great body.

The sounds came from inside Lippe. The processes of
decay had begun – the shift of fluids, the expansion of
gases, the slow settling of the body masses – and deep
intestinal rumblings and muffled gastric explosions came
intermittently from the soft chambers and labyrinths of
flesh. The detonations merged together, grew louder as
they travelled through the body into the gullet, and
rattled in the throat. Unsupported by a dental plate, the
puckered upper lip had sunk back into the gaping
mouth; now it fluttered outwards before a rush of cold
air. The flatulence of death. Dilke turned his back
against it with a grimace of disgust and walked into the
tangled carpet fibres.

The way to the skirting board was blocked by Lippe's
outstretched arm, forcing Dilke along a direct line to the
door.

Glimpsed through the forest of nylon tufts, the long
line of Schmidt's body, and the blunt curves of the
American's great buttocks and the Negro's belly, seemed

more terrestrial than human. To Dilke they were three mountain ranges: one in lightweight Dacron, one in pinstripe, one in starched white linen, and the carpet was a flat green valley between them. As he got nearer to them their shapes and dimensions slowly changed until a tangle of colossal legs loomed high above him and obscured the torsos he had seen from far away.

Botticelli was slumped across Kirangozi, and Schmidt lay stretched out against the southern wall of the room.

The valley between the German's body and the two others became narrower as Dilke travelled along it; at last he reached a gap a few inches wide – a score or so micro-feet – with the overhanging folds of a laboratory coat on one side and a monolithic presidential shoe, its polished toe pointed upwards, on the other.

He had smelled blood in the valley, now the smell was overpowering. He climbed a piece of broken crockery and saw two vast lakes of blood spread across the carpet before him with only a narrow space separating them. Afraid that they would flow together and bar his way, Dilke jumped down and hurried between the viscid walls of blood, which moved as thickly and slowly as cooling lava.

When he was clear he looked back across the reeking lakes.

Botticelli's face and head were bruised and lacerated by his victim's fists and jewelled rings, and juice from his shredded cigar glazed his chin. Beyond the curve of Kirangozi's black cheek his tongue protruded obscenely between swollen lips. Schmidt's face was turned to the wall.

PART FIVE

18

Dilke lay on his bunk exhausted by his journey back to the Aid.

Lippe was dead, but joy was absent from Dilke's heart. He felt only a great emptiness.

And now that Lippe was dead?

Dilke closed his eyes wearily and tried to think of the future. Until now total preoccupation with investigation and revenge had left no room for other thoughts; now nausea and lethargy, the delayed effects of the gas, made coherent thought impossible.

The minutes passed; he lay half-asleep; then two words floated up from the depths of his subconscious: *Telephone Jebb.*

Nausea forgotten, Dilke left his bunk and hurried to the files. His Excellency was in the *Who's Who*. The embassy number in Lima and his residence outside the city were both listed.

Dilke left the Aid and entered the dark interior of the desk phone; he removed the recorder which he had attached to the miniature telephone hook-up five days before, and he dialled the embassy.

There was no answer – it was Saturday; but he got a reply from the residence. Above the noise of laughter a woman called, 'It's for you, darling.'

After a pause, a man lazily enquired, 'Yes?'

'Is that Sir James Jebb?'

The voice gave a languid affirmation.

'This is an emergency and is confidential. Is it safe to speak?'

'Who is speaking, please?'

'My name is Dilke. We met in Lord Raglen's office in February. I am speaking from the offices of Compañía Peruana de Plásticos.'

'One moment!' There was another pause, then the party noises were cut off and Jebb spoke more briskly on another line.

'Say that again, please.'

'I am Captain Mathew Dilke, you met me in Lord Raglen's office with the agent Gilbert Bellamy before we came out here to investigate Professor Heinrich Lippe. Bellamy is dead, and I am in Lippe's office at this moment. Lippe is also dead. There has been bloody war here. I want you to come here now, Sir James, and pick me up ...'

'My God! We thought you were both dead. Bellamy was found ...'

Dilke cut in, 'Come alone. Tell no one. Walk straight in and take the lift to the top floor. Go down the corridor facing you and pass through a door, then enter the first room on your left. I'll be in the blue hearing-aid on the desk.'

'I'll come immediately.'

'A guard has run amok, but he'll have simmered down by now ...' The line was dead before the sentence was finished.

Dilke was waiting in the Aid's viewing chair when the ambassador arrived.

He called to him over the speaker and Sir James hurried to the desk and blinked down at him. Jebb had seen into the conference room in his search for Lippe's office and his voice shook. 'God almighty! What has happened here?'

Dilke had had time to work things out: Jebb must report the deaths to the police. He could say he found the bodies when calling on Lippe about matters concerning Bellamy ...

Sir James did not demur, and he was suitably distraught when he rang the police.

Before the cavalcade arrived with sirens and slamming car doors, Dilke told as much of what had happened as he thought an ambassador should know.

Then the place swarmed with armed police. They looked into the conference room, then kicked open the door to the main lab where they found the guard slumped, weeping, amongst the dead laboratory staff.

Dilke spent two days on a desk in Sir James Jebb's private study in the ambassadorial residence. Jebb arranged with Whitehall that he would take Dilke back to England himself, and also arranged the carriage home of Gilbert Bellamy's body.

Bellamy's death had been headline news in English and Peruvian papers – Jebb showed Dilke back copies from the embassy file.

Now it was *yesterday's* news; as cold as Boxing Day turkey. Dilke saw, tucked away on an inside page of *The Times*, a short postscript to the affair.

PIGSTY SLAYING VICTIM TO BE FLOWN HOME. The body of murdered British businessman, 54-year-old Mr Gilbert Francis Bellamy, who was found stabbed in a pigsty in a village thirty miles east of Lima, has been released by Peruvian police authorities for transportation back to England. A communiqué states that Mr Bellamy may have died resisting an attempt to kidnap him, or have been the target for political assassination by Marxist/Leninist terrorists. Police investigations are suspended due to lack of information.

19

Bellamy was flying home as cargo.

Dilke coldly watched the long box slide into the hold of the big jet from his place of concealment in Sir James's breast pocket, and saw the porters cross themselves mechanically as they closed and locked the doors.

The ambassador signed consignment papers and returned them with a smile, and a word, which was lost in the whistle of the jet engines, to the freight officer. Then he climbed the boarding steps and was taken to his seat in the forward cabin where a hostess brought him newspapers and magazines and took his order for dinner.

El Peruano was still running the plastics factory mass-murder story on its front page; printing columns of journalistic surmise about the killer's motives beneath pictures of his nine victims. The ambassador lit a monogrammed cigarette and sat back to read every word.

Dilke had been incommunicado since the ambassador had dressed for the journey. Sir James had pushed the earplug and cable to the bottom of his breast pocket before clipping the Aid into place, and had tucked a display handkerchief behind the Aid, in a matching colour.

A fold of blue silk had fallen across the observation dome and obscured Dilke's view of the cabin, but he could see clearly through the cabin window.

The plane moved, then rapidly gathered speed. Dilke watched the tarmac and the yellow runway lights flash past; the machine rose steeply, banked sharply over the airport, and flew inland.

As they gained height their speed seemed to decrease until they appeared hardly to move at all. Far below, in the purple evening shadows which covered the wooded foothills, a tiny circle of water reflected the blue sky. Dilke watched it sombrely until it disappeared behind the curved edge of the cabin window, then he looked up towards the sunlit crests ahead.

They crossed the mountains through a twelve thousand foot gap between snow-covered peaks. The whole continent east of the Andes was in darkness. Shreds of cloud flitted past the window, then the plane flew through a wall of vapour and entered a transient and ethereal world.

Mountains of cumulus edged with golden light towered above oceans of grey stratus, and tiny white clouds dotted the sky between. Through the bottom of a vast whirlpool in the sea of cloud the dark substantial earth and the winking lights of a small town were visible miles below. Dilke glimpsed them briefly before the plane flew into a valley between banks of cloud. The eastern side of the valley glimmered in the last light of day; pink and violet shadows coloured the opposing slope.

Mathew Dilke was moved by the melancholy beauty of it all. A small irregularity on the shadowed face of the cloud could have been a solitary house, a cottage overlooking a lonely valley. The sky above the exquisite, weightless landscape was now a deep, deep blue and full of stars.

Cruising at forty thousand feet the engine noise was minimal. Dilke heard a murmur of voices from the seats behind; then he saw (between the overhanging fold of the handkerchief and the ambassador's opened newspaper) a smart uniform skirt appear, and two slim hands holding a pencil and notepad.

'I hope you are enjoying your flight, Your Excellency.' The girl spoke with practised sincerity. 'Would you care for an aperitif before dinner?'

Sir James asked for a Bloody Mary and gave up reading when his drink arrived.

The Bloody Mary preceded a bottle of Volnay, which accompanied avocado mousse, steak à la moutarde, and flummery Drambuie.

Dilke watched a steady traffic of food and wine pass between Sir James's lips, and listened to the mild flirtation he conducted between courses with the Peruvian hostess, against the background of subdued talk and laughter which accompanies dining-out anywhere in the world. Only the brown paper bags, tucked discreetly into pockets on the backs of the seats, hinted at the precarious equilibrium of the dining-room.

The cabin was hot by English standards. The ambassador slid off his jacket, carefully hung it on the plastic wall hook next to his seat and sat back contentedly with his brandy.

Dilke's view of cabin and night sky was replaced by a close-up of the smooth vinyl-covered cabin-wall. He unclipped his harness and went below. The steady vibration of the plane and the gentle swaying of the jacket had replaced the ambassador's sharp and irregular movements.

The Aid's bill-of-fare did not match the plane's cuisine. But Dilke was not hungry.

He sat on his bunk and stared at the sheet of paper he had stuck on the wall on the night he got drunk, and he read the words out loud. 'For all guilt is punished on earth.'

Goethe had got it only half right!

Heinrich Lippe was dead, but so was Bellamy. He reached out and took down the paper and slowly tore it into two, four, eight, sixteen, thirty-two and, with a grunt, sixty-four fragments and dropped them on the floor.

The job was finished.

He should start writing his report soon.

He did not feel like writing.

He went to the cupboard and took out a bottle and a glass.